Reviews

Tell Us a Sick One Jakey
'This book is quite repulsive!' Sir Michael Havers, Attorney General

Never Alone with Rex Malone
'A ribald, ambitious black comedy, a story powerfully told.' *The Daily Mail*

'I was absolutely flabbergasted when I read it!' Robert Maxwell

The Ruin of Jesse Cavendish
'Eleanor Berry is to Literature what Hieronymous Bosch is to Art. As with all Miss Berry's books, the reader has a burning urge to turn the page.' *International Continental Review*

Your Father Died an the Gallows
'A unique display of black humour which somehow fails to depress the reader.' Craig McLittle, *The Rugby Gazette*

Cap'n Bob and Me
'One of the most amusing books I have read for a long time. Eleanor Berry is an original.' Elisa Seagrave, *The Literary Review*

'Undoubtedly the most amusing book I have read all year.' Julia Llewellyn Smith, *The Times*

'A comic masterpiece.' *The Times*

Seamus O'Rafferty and Dr Blenkinsop
'A riotous read from start to finish.' Ned McMurphy,
The Dublin Times

Alandra Varinia, Seed of Sarah
'Eleanor Berry manages to maintain her raw and
haunting wit as much as ever.' Dwight C. Farr, *The
Texas Chronicle*

Jaxton the Silver Boy
'This time Eleanor Berry tries her versatile hand at
politics. Her sparkling wit and the reader's desire to
turn the page are still in evidence. Eleanor Berry is
unique.' Don F. Saunderson, *The South London Review*

Someone's Been Done Up Harley
'In her tenth book, Eleanor Berry's dazzling wit hits
the Harley Street scene yet again. Her extraordinary
humour had me in stitches.' Thelma Masters, *The
Oxford Voice*

O Hitman, My Hitman!
'Eleanor Berry's volatile pen is at it again. This time,
she takes her readers back to the humorously eccentric
Harley Sweet community. She also introduces Romany
gypsies and travelling circuses, a trait she has inherited
from her self-confessed gypsy aunt, the late writer,
Eleanor Smith, after whom she is named. Like Smith,
Berry is an inimitable and delightfully natural writer.'
Kev Gein, *Johannesburg Evening Sketch*

McArandy was Hanged on the Gibbet High
'We have here a potboiling, swashbuckling blockbuster,

which is rich in adventure, intrigue, history, amorous episodes and black humour. The story Eleanor Berry tells is multi-coloured, multi-faceted and nothing short of fantastic.' Angel Z. Hogan, *The Daily Melbourne Times*

The Scourging of Poor Little Maggie
'This harrowing, tragic and deeply ennobling book caused me to weep for two days after reading it.' Moira McClusky, *The Cork Evening News*

The Revenge of Miss Rhoda Buckleshott
'Words are Eleanor Berry's toys and her use of them is boundless.' Mary Hickman, professional historian and writer

The Most Singular Adventures of Eddy Vernon
'Rather a hot book for bedtime.' Nigel Dempster, *The Daily Mail*

The Maniac in Room 14
'This is the funniest book I've read for months.' Samantha Morris, *The Exeter Daily News*

Stop the Car, Mr Becket!
'This book makes for fascinating reading, as strange and entertaining as Eleanor Berry's sixteen books which came out before it.' Gaynor Evans, *Bristol Evening Post*

Take it Away, It's Red
'Despite the sometimes weighty portent of this book, a sense of subtle, dry and powerfully engaging humour reigns throughout its pages. The unexpected twist is stupendous.' Stephen Carson, *The Carolina Sun*

THE HOUSE OF THE WEIRD DOCTORS

Eleanor Berry

www.eleanorberry.net

Book Guild Publishing
Sussex, England

First published in Great Britain in 2005 by
The Book Guild Ltd
25 High Street
Lewes, East Sussex
BN7 2LU

Typesetting in Baskerville by
Keyboard Services, Luton, Bedfordshire

Printed in Great Britain by
Athenaeum Press Ltd, Gateshead

A catalogue record for this book is available from
The British Library

ISBN 1 85776 913 9

For Betty

The date was 3rd September, 1985. The time had just turned 9.00 a.m.

On the floor of the majestic hallway in the Royal Society of Medicine in Wimpole Street, London, a dead man lay, his skull brutally crushed and his brains scattered on the polished marble floor.

By his head, lay a mace, the kind used during the Spanish Inquisition, a heavy, spiked, metal ball on a chain.

An array of oil paintings of physicians of a bygone age peered cynically and austerely down upon this man.

To an observer, their faces could have seemed complacent, cold-blooded and almost gloating at the butchered man's demise.

A sophisticated observer, however, might have assumed that these doctors felt obliged to appear solemn, serene and obstinately dour of feature, to enable the viewers of the paintings to regard them with the reverence that qualified doctors, irrespective of their misdemeanours, command of the layman.

The first person to enter the building that morning was the receptionist, Mrs Elsa Rose, a middle-aged, grey-haired, obese woman of unprepossessing appearance and hysterical temperament.

When she had stopped screaming (indeed her screams lasted for three minutes), her trembling hand reached for the telephone and she dialled 999.

The police arrived within 20 minutes. They were Detective Inspector Massey, a robustly-built, rude, bald man, and his short, stout colleague whose title was Detective Constable Bush.

1

Massey seized the tannoy from Mrs Rose's desk and made an announcement which reverberated round the building.

'This is a police announcement. Will everyone in the building refrain from leaving until further notice.'

At 10.15 a.m. before the body was encased in a polythene bag and removed, a police photographer arrived on the scene accompanied by a forensic scientist who made a brief preliminary examination. The dead man had no injuries on his face or the front of his body. The forensic scientist estimated that he had been taken unawares from behind and had been unable to face his attacker to defend himself.

The photographer took pictures of the body from all angles, while the forensic scientist, a down-to-earth man called Dick Bullet, looked on.

'Looks like his head's been bashed in by a battleship,' he remarked.

He and the photographer noticed that the injuries had been caused by a spiked object, namely the mace which lay by the dead man's side.

Once the body had been taken outside, the occupants of the building were summoned by the tannoy and told to assemble in the hall, and not to leave the building, until their names, addresses and identities had been taken.

The time was 10.30 a.m. Only 30 people were present, but Bush felt irritated at having to take all their names and addresses down and match them with their identities, as well as having to ask for a bucket of hot water and a cloth to clear up the mess the killer had made.

2

It had been established, following a search of the possessions the dead man carried, that his name was Frederick Ruttershields, a professor of medicine. It was evident that he was a man of considerable wealth. He had on a neatly ironed, pin-striped suit, a black and white, striped tie, shoes of original crocodile hide, and carried a gold cigarette case on which the words 'To darling F from your faithful T' were engraved.

Detective Constable Bush examined the dead man's wallet for clues, a task he regretted doing due to the abundance of rolled-up pieces of paper, all of which could be relevant and had to be examined.

At the bottom of Ruttershields's wallet he found a picture of a young man with an earring through his right ear lobe and a tiger-patterned punk haircut. The man bore no physical resemblance to the deceased and there were no photographs of women or children either.

Massey turned the photograph over and found an almost illegible message, written in a hurry. The texture of the photograph suggested it had been taken recently.

Rutty, baby, who catches while I pitch (Sssh!) and for whom I ache as soon as you can make it.

Rutty, I'm psychic and I know they are after you because of the very thing you possess. I'll refer to it as 'The Thing'.

Don't go home, tonight, Rutty-bear. They know your wife's address. Come to me tonight. Come to my place. They won't find you there.

I love you, baby – from Tiger.

'What do you make of this, Bush?' asked Massey. 'It doesn't tell us much. What do you think was in his possession which was so vital to the killer?'

'How should I know? Apart from his name, Tiger's not much to go on either.'

Bush looked through Ruttershields's wallet again and realised he had missed further equally important evidence.

> *Freddie, dear, please find some time to take off from your precious work to come and see me and the children.*
>
> *You go away for weeks at a time without coming to see us.*
>
> *Freddie, what's going on? I know you're hiding 'You Know What' so obsessively that I feel someone will come round to kill me and the children.*
>
> *Please tell us where you are, Freddie. We won't tell. Sheila.*

'It says here the address is 85 Clinton Grove, Hampstead,' said Bush.

'That's our first port of call. We'll go there and break the news and see if there are other clues as to what this man Ruttershields had in his possession.'

The time was 1.15 p.m. Detective Inspector Massey went to 85 Clinton Grove, Hampstead, accompanied by Detective Constable Bush, to see Mrs Ruttershields. Bush rang the bell which was answered by a woman wearing a mauve blouse tucked into a long, black skirt, secured by a matching, black, leather belt. She looked like a Mogadon capsule. A gold pendant hung

4

round her neck and she wore numerous rings on each hand. Her long dark hair was drawn on top of her head.

'Mrs T Ruttershields?' said Massey.

'I am not Mrs T Ruttershields. My name is Sheila Ruttershields.' She raised her voice shrilly and asked, 'Has someone had an accident?'

'There's more to it than that,' said Massey. 'May we come in?'

Sheila looked cowed but not terrified.

'Please do. I've nothing to offer you. What's happened?'

'I'm afraid I have tragic news for you, Mrs Ruttershields.'

The woman went pale as if about to faint.

'Is it one of the children?'

'No. It's your husband. He was found dead this morning in the hall of the Royal Society of Medicine. He was battered to death.'

Mrs Ruttershields's expression showed relief that neither of her children, Marius, aged 18, and Miriam, aged eleven, had been harmed, but her eyes filled with tears at the prospect of breaking the news to them.

'Mrs Ruttershields, much though this may distress you, there are further questions I have to ask you,' said Massey.

'Yes?'

'When did you last see your late husband?'

'It's been three months now. We're separated but not divorced.'

'Where are your children?'

'At their schools. I'm not due to collect them until 4.30.'

Suddenly, she burst into tears, wishing she didn't have to tell them.

'I understand how distressing this is for you but we are going to have to ask you some very harrowing questions,' said Massey.

He handed her the photograph of the man who called himself 'Tiger'.

'Do you know who this is?' asked Massey.

'He's a friend of my son, Marius. I last saw him two years ago when he was invited to our house.'

Massey turned the photograph over and showed her the message on the back.

Strangely, she did not look particularly shocked.

'I separated from my husband when I discovered he was a homosexual, and I found his liaison with a friend of my son unacceptable. I packed all his belongings and threw them out into the street, but I always let him come back to visit us. In fact, I encouraged him to.'

Bush turned his face away from the widow and gave a watery smile. Massey was too busy questioning her to notice.

'I want to ask you a question about this message on the back of this photograph, Mrs Ruttershields. Reference is made to parties intending to harm your husband because of something he owned.'

Massey pulled out the other relevant items related to the case and showed Mrs Ruttershields the letter she had written to her husband dated two weeks before his death.

'You refer to "You Know What". Does that refer to his homosexuality?'

'Of course not. I've known about that ever since we separated, as I told you before.'

'Can you remember what it was you were referring to?'

'Yes,' she said hesitantly.

'Well, what is it?'

'It's something I can't reveal.'

'I have his address book here,' said Massey. 'For a Professor of Medicine there are some pretty insalubrious addresses in it. Do you know Tim from Earls Court?'

'No. I've never heard of him.'

'Churchill Knightsbridge from Brixton? Sounds like a coloured gentleman to me.'

'I don't know him.'

'Cuthbert Scantlebury from Lewisham?'

'No.'

Massey read out a long list of names of people living at rough addresses, men and women alike. Mrs Ruttershields hadn't heard of any of them.

'Did your husband go with women as well as men?'

'Yes. He was bisexual. I wouldn't have minded if he'd only gone with women. It was the fact that he went with men that was so distressing.'

Massey read out the names of the 30 people called forward in the Royal Society of Medicine, some doctors, some researchers, some medical students. Mrs Ruttershields was not familiar with any of these names.

She knew a few of the doctors listed in her

husband's address book. Sometimes, he had invited them to dinner and they were well-known to her. Apart from that, she was unable to help the police further with their enquiries.

Massey continued, 'Mrs Ruttershields, we will have to call your children home from school.'

Marius and Miriam were brought home and told the news of their father's death. They calmed down a little after being given a glass of water each.

'Does the name "Tiger" mean anything to you, lad?' Massey asked Marius.

'Yes, he's an old friend. I haven't seen him for some time. Is he hurt?'

'No, lad, he's not hurt. Your mother told me he was a friend of yours. Have you got his address?'

Puzzled, Marius pulled out a small, red leather address book and found Tiger's address.

Massey looked even more bemused. Tiger lived at 289 Albany Road, Camberwell. At that time, most of the houses in that road were squats.

'Why do you want to find Tiger?' asked Marius.

'Because he was, I believe, a friend of your family and we have to eliminate him from our enquiries.'

Massey and Bush arrived on Tiger's doorstep at 3.00 p.m. A squatter opened the door. Eight other squatters occupied the same house, which was filthy. Old bags of rubbish were thrown over the bannisters into the hall, since no one had bothered to carry them out of the building for collection.

The door was opened by a tramp with rust-coloured

hair and rings through his ears and nose. He was white and his face was covered with disfiguring acne.

'Does a man called Tiger live here?' asked Massey.

The man, who could hardly stand up straight, due to intoxication with drink and drugs, leant precariously against the door-post.

'Yeah, Tiger's here. He's shooting up.'

'What do you mean, he's shooting up?'

'He's gettin' nice an' high.'

There was a narrow limit to Massey's patience.

'I don't care whether he's getting high or not. Bring him downstairs!'

The man who came down had the same almond-shaped green eyes as in the photograph, and a pointed nose. His short hair was bleached a yellowish blond with prominent dark tiger stripes. He wore frayed blue jeans which were stiff with dirt, a T-shirt bearing the words 'Avoid hangovers. Stay drunk' and a torn, black, leather jacket, also engrained with filth.

'Are you known as Tiger?' asked Massey.

The young man's retinas were so clouded over with drugs that he looked blind. He remained in the same position, leaning against the door post, rhythmically chewing gum. Eventually he answered.

'Yeah.'

'What's your real name?'

'Edmund Henry Jenkins.'

'This your photograph?'

'Yeah.'

'I gather you've been a friend of Frederick Ruttershields's.'

'Yes. Is he all right?'

'He's dead.'

'Dead? I ... don't understand.'

Jenkins fainted but Bush broke his fall. After two minutes or so, he came round.

'Get me water.'

Bush mounted the perilously shaky, unbannistered staircase and entered a filthy bathroom. The lavatory was blocked to the rim with human waste and the squatters had been using the bath to urinate in. Bush found a chipped cup above the unused basin and filled it with water before going down to Jenkins.

'Drink this,' he commanded, his voice cold and betraying no emotion. 'Sit down and listen carefully. Frederick Ruttershields was found dead in the hall of the Royal Society of Medicine. It is estimated he had been dead for several hours. When we found him he was already in rigor. He had been battered to death.'

After drinking the water, Jenkins was more composed. Massey showed him the note on the back of the photograph.

'You refer to "the very thing that you possess". What is that thing?'

Jenkins burst into tears.

'I don't know. He wouldn't tell me.'

'You also made it plain that you pitched and he caught. That's not a particularly elegant thing to say, is it?'

'I'm allowed to say what I want when I write to a friend.'

'Nevertheless, we would like you to accompany us

to the police station so that we can eliminate you from our enquiries.'

Jenkins began to get cold turkey once at the police station. It went on for several hours. Bush gave him some tea.

'Got a fag on you?' asked Jenkins.

Bush gave him a cigarette and lit it. Jenkins felt more relaxed once he had inhaled.

Detective Sergeant Bixby, a somewhat ridiculous-looking man with whiskers, and the only member of staff at the police station to carry an unused whistle, took over from Massey. He effected a bogus upper-class accent, using gimmicky H's when they were not warranted.

'How long had you known Professor Frederick Ruttershields?' he asked.

'Two years.'

'How did you meet him?'

'I went to school with his son, Marius. Me and Marius were both sixteen. I didn't drop out until after I left school. I had no incentive to work because I had benefit and was able to squat instead of getting rented lodgings. When I wanted money for smack, I went on the sodding game, didn't I?'

'Mr Jenkins, I don't require a long, rambling account of your lifestyle. How did you come to be on intimate terms with the late Frederick Ruttershields?'

'Give us another fag, Guv.'

Bixby got out his packet of cigarettes and threw one at Jenkins, together with a box of matches. Jenkins lit up, his hands trembling.

11

'I got a scholarship to the school. I couldn't afford the fees otherwise. I was born in the East End of London and grew up there.

'Once at the school, I had this great opportunity to get in with the toffs. I had ambitions in them days and dreams of bunging myself into Oxford. I even spoke with a toff's accent. I wanted to find a place in a toff's home, to give myself a bit of status like.

'So I got locked on to this posh boy called Marius Ruttershields. Always at the top of the class he was, and captain at cricket. I sucked up to him, like, telling him jokes all the time and making him laugh.

'One day he said, "Why don't you come home this weekend? My parents would like to meet you."'

Here, he intimated an upper class accent.

'"Blimey," I thought. "Here's your chance. Go for it." I got my hair cut and got myself all togged up. I even got a younger boy to lend me his fancy, ostentatious watch. A proper little toff I was.'

Bixby crossed and uncrossed his legs.

'Mr Jenkins, would you kindly get to the point.'

'I'm about to, Guv. Give us a chance. So old Marius took me to this huge house. Covered with them old masters, it was, fancy silver, bloomin' ceramic vases, the lot!

'I arrived at the house just before lunch at 1.00 p.m.

'"Tiger," Marius said, "may I introduce you to my father?"

'I was about to say, "Charmed, I'm sure," but I thought that might sound daft.

' "How do you do, Professor Ruttershields?" I said.

'Then I suddenly noticed what he looked like. He had this beautiful, slicked-back, silvery hair and his eyes were azure blue, like the sea off one of them islands the darkies come from.

'It wasn't just that. He stared straight into my eyes and gave me what I thought was a Mafia handshake.'

'How do you know what a Mafia handshake's like?' barked Bixby.

'Seen it in the movies, ain't I?'

'What actually did he do when he shook your hand?'

'It seemed like there was a look of love in his eyes. I couldn't look anywhere else. I knew from then on I adored him. When he shook my hand, he held it tight; then he tickled the palm of my hand with his finger.'

'Sounds more like a homosexual handshake than a Mafia handshake. Had you had any homosexual experiences before?' asked Bixby.

'No, but once I saw this man it was like being hypnotised. I wanted to get up him like a rat up a drainpipe.'

'There's no need to be vulgar,' said Bixby. 'I gather you saw him again.'

'Yeah, I did and all,' said Jenkins. 'He used to take me to a bedroom at the Royal Society of Medicine most afternoons. You should have seen us. We was at it like bleedin' rabbits.'

Bixby ran his hand through his dark brown hair.

'How many times did you see him?'

'So many, I've lost count.'

13

'Are you saying you were as intimate as that, without him telling you anything about his work?'

'No. He never talked shop with me – not about medicine. I don't know nothing about it. All he said was that he had something in his possession which was so vital that other doctors would have been prepared to kill him to get it.'

'And you have no idea whatsoever what that thing was or who these doctors were?'

'No.'

Bixby turned round in his swivel chair, utterly frustrated.

'I'm going to read you out a list of names. They may be people you know.'

'Go on, then.'

'Tim from Earls Court?'

'I know him vaguely but not his address. He pedals smack in the Underground.'

'What about a man called Churchill Knightsbridge from Brixton?'

Jenkins lit another cigarette.

'Oh, Church. He lives in the squat with me and the others now. He was in the crapper when your pals came round to fetch me.'

'Is he a homosexual?'

'Yeah. We all are in the squat.'

'Was Churchill Knightsbridge known to the Ruttershields family?'

Jenkins was still feeling uncomfortable through want of heroin. He crossed and uncrossed his legs.

'Course not, stupid! Can you imagine a bunch of toffs taking in a bleedin' black?'

14

'So you're saying for certain that Churchill not only knew nothing of Ruttershields but had no idea of his existence?'

'I don't think he knew him. He may have mentioned him.'

'Does the name Cuthbert Scantlebury mean anything to you?' asked Bixby.

'Yeah. Cuthbert's in the squat with us. He was upstairs rolling about with cold turkey when you called. I don't think he knew Rutty, either.'

Bixby stood up.

'You've told me what I need to know for the time being, but I will probably have to call you in again. It will also be necessary to interview the people you know.'

Even though his withdrawal symptoms were almost gone, Jenkins still felt cramp in his stomach. He staggered to his feet.

'OK, guv,' he muttered.

The following day, the police called for Churchill Knightsbridge.

The questioning technique was almost identical to that used with Jenkins, the only difference being that when Knightsbridge walked into the questioning room, he beamed theatrically, 'I greet you in the wonderful name of Jesus!' and left Bixby flabbergasted.

'Does the name Frederick Ruttershields mean anything to you?'

'Yeah. Tiger Jenkins bangs on about him non-stop. He calls him "Rutty".'

15

'What has he told you about Rutty?'

'He just bangs on and on about him being such a beautiful and wonderful person who has got something someone else wants.'

Bixby sat up straight in his chair.

'Did he not say what that thing was?'

'No. He said this man Rutty wouldn't tell him.'

'But you did say Jenkins talked about him all the time.'

'It's true he did, but all he talked about was his ass which he said was like a ripe mango, man.'

Cuthbert Scantlebury was the next person to help the police with their enquiries. He was completely bald with a swastika tattooed on top of his head. He was well-built and formidable-looking with a knuckleduster on his right hand and his left hand was covered with a foul-smelling, festering wound which looked gangrenous.

He arrived at the police station bare-chested and wearing frayed denim shorts and bovver boots.

'Mr Scantlebury, had you ever met Frederick Ruttershields?' asked Bixby.

'For Christ's sake give me a break from hearing about Frederick Ruttershields! It's all I ever hear about. I'm fed up with it, man!'

'Do you know he had in his possession something other people wanted?'

'Course, I did.'

'What was it?'

'I don't know, do I?'

'Did Tiger Jenkins know?'

'No. The man probably never told him.'

'Have you any idea who killed Frederick Ruttershields?'

'I don't know and I don't care,' said Scantlebury.

Massey and Bush visited Ruttershields's Harley Street address the following day. Massey approached the receptionist and showed him his card.

'I have to see Frederick Ruttershields's secretary to ask her a few questions.'

'Third floor on your right.'

The secretary was wearing a black miniskirt with a yellow shirt tucked in.

'Are you Frederick Ruttershields's secretary?' asked Massey.

The woman smiled sarcastically.

'I'm only a temp. Ruth Shenton's the permanent secretary.'

'How can I find her?'

'I'm afraid I don't know. She was so badly affected by the murder that she was admitted to hospital with shock.'

'What's the name of the hospital?'

The temp became aggressive.

'I haven't the faintest idea and even if I did, I wouldn't tell you. You can't just storm into a hospital to cross-examine a woman with that kind of complaint.'

Massey decided to get rough.

'Would you give me the name of your agency please, miss.'

The temp fed a top copy and two carbons into her typewriter.

'I don't have to give you the name of my agency because you're not hiring me,' she said and went on typing.

Massey pulled the plug out of her typewriter.

'Perhaps you'd care to tell me now.'

'I can tell you nothing because I know nothing. I've never met Frederick Ruttershields and I don't know anything about his work.'

Massey went up close to her.

'Whose work are you doing if you don't know anything about his work?'

'I'm doing some tapes dating back to a month ago. I was called in to do the backlog.'

'Do you mind if we listen to some of these tapes?'

'Sorry, my administrator told me not to divulge such information. It's private and confidential.'

'Rules have to be broken in murder cases, young lady. Who's your supervisor?'

'I'll take you along to her. She's next door but one. Her name's Henrietta Jones.'

'Thank you.'

The temp took the police into the administrator's office.

'I had to bring them to you, Henrietta,' she said, 'as they want me to divulge information I was told was confidential, about the late Mr Ruttershields.'

'You were right to bring them here. It was most professional of you.'

She turned to the police.

'Won't you take a seat? What can I do for you?'

Massey sat back in his chair and crossed his legs.

'We want to know exactly what Professor Ruttershields had in his possession which other members of the medical profession urgently needed.'

The administrator had some idea but lied to the police for reasons of ethics. She had been devoted to Professor Ruttershields.

She sat on the remaining chair, crossed her legs and lit a cigarette.

'Why money, I should imagine. Who doesn't need that urgently?'

'Don't fool about, Mrs Jones. We know it wasn't money.'

'Then I'm sorry, I really can't help you.'

'Was the man well-liked?'

'Yes, on the surface. He was reasonably affable, but underneath that, he kept himself to himself. I simply can't understand why anyone would want to kill him.'

Massey was becoming frustrated. Bush looked bored.

Massey said, 'Mind if we listen to these tapes?'

'No, sorry, that is strictly against protocol. Besides, I dictated them and they are private letters. You won't find what you're looking for in any of them.'

'Do you know where Ruth, the permanent secretary, is?'

'She's in a lunatic asylum.'

'Which one?'

'The Maudsley in Denmark Hill, Camberwell. You won't get much out of her. She's extremely ill.'

'How ill?'

19

Henrietta lost her temper.

'How should I know how ill she is? She's got a mental illness. That really is all I can tell you.'

'Thank you for your trouble, Mrs Jones. We may have to come back.'

Massey hated the idea of having to go into a lunatic asylum. The experience reminded him of having to visit his schizophrenic sister who jumped out of a sixth-floor window to her death.

He and Bush strode into the Maudsley. Massey flashed his warrant at the woman manning the enquiries desk.

'What ward is Ruth Shenton on?' he asked aggressively.

He wanted to get this enquiry over and done with as soon as possible.

The woman, a heavily made-up, old spinster, who obviously loathed her job, turned on a green and black, flickering screen and pushed a series of buttons.

'Aubrey Lewis, third floor,' she said.

Massey was in too bad a temper to say 'thank you'. Neither he nor Bush could find the lift, so they mounted the stairs to the third floor and made for the Aubrey Lewis ward.

Massey became profoundly depressed by the sights he saw before him, and as the Charge Nurse couldn't keep his eye on everyone at once, lesbianism, some-times involving flabby, elderly women with suppurating bedsores, was rife.

A feeling of nausea overwhelmed Massey and

this, together with the memory he had of his sister, threw him into a depression which increased his rage.

'Can I help you?' asked the Charge Nurse, a tall, lean man in his thirties with rust-coloured hair.

'Yeah. Detective Inspector Massey, I've a warrant to interview Ruth Shenton.'

Charge Nurse Jessop was equally as depressed by his surroundings as Massey and almost as short-tempered.

'I'm Charge Nurse Jessop. You are certainly going to do nothing of the kind. Ruth Shenton's in Intensive Care.'

'Intensive Care? Intensive-bloody-Care? Take me there this instant!'

Jessop tried to block Massey's path.

'Now look here, constable...' he began.

'I'm not a constable! I'm a Detective Inspector!'

Massey and Bush strode through the ward, taking care not to look at the patients for fear of joining them. They followed the signs to Intensive Care.

This time, they were intercepted by two female nurses. There were only four patients there, three of whom were unconscious with heart and brain monitors. Ruth Shenton was the only one who wasn't unconscious.

'Detective Inspector Massey!' barked Massey, flashing his warrant.

'You can't come in here!' began one of the nurses.

Massey brushed past the nurse. He and Bush made for Ruth Shenton's bed which had a label at the end of it saying who she was.

'Miss Shenton,' began Massey with uncharacteristic gentleness.

'Yes.'

Her voice was faint and her speech slurred because of the drugs she was on.

'I'm sorry to come to you when you're not at all well. You've probably heard about Professor Ruttershields's untimely death.'

Ruth showed only the whites of her eyes and made a harrowing groaning noise.

'Miss Shenton?'

'Yes.'

'You know how he died, don't you?'

Ruth screwed her top sheet into a ball and started shaking.

'You were his secretary and personal assistant, weren't you?'

'Yes.'

'Take your time. Just tell me one more thing: what was it Professor Ruttershields possessed that so many other doctors wanted?'

Ruth rubbed her hands up and down the sheet and her eyes rolled back again.

'It was, it was...'

'Yes,' said Massey patiently. 'Tell us what it was?'

'It was oz, oz, oze.'

'What? I can't understand you.'

'Oz, oz, oz, oz, oze...'

She fell unconscious. Later that day, she died of a brain haemorrhage.

Massey and Bush got into their Panda car parked outside the hospital.

22

'What do you think she meant?' asked Massey.
'I've no idea.'
'Just oz, oz, oz, oze, is not enough to go on. We've wasted all this time and for nothing.'
'I was just thinking,' remarked Bush, 'she could have been referring to the ozone layer in the sky that lets in cancerous rays.'
Massey changed gear impatiently, grinding the clutch.
'Don't be daft, Bush! How the hell can a man be in possession of a hole in the bloody sky? If you can't think of anything intelligent to say, keep your mouth shut.'

The cook in the Ruttershields household was the next person to be interviewed by Massey and his colleague. Her name was Florry Shanks and she was even more peculiar than her name.
When the police arrived, Sheila Ruttershields opened the door.
'We need to interview your cook,' said Massey.
'I don't think she's very presentable. Can I ask her to go up and change first? She's something of an oddity.'
'It's all right. I don't mind what she's wearing. Bring her in.'
Mrs Ruttershields rang a bell on the wall. Florry walked into the room with a pronounced limp.
She had on a tartan scarf secured in a gypsy's knot at the back of her head, a brown and purple striped overall, blue and white striped tights and

bovver boots. She had beady black eyes, an aquiline nose and bright red lipstick. She was about 40 years of age and looked brutally eccentric.

'You rang for me, madam?'

'Yes. The police want you to help them with their enquiries regarding my husband's death. I'll leave you in the living room to talk.'

'How long have you worked for your employers?' Massey asked Florry.

Before she answered the question, she took a bottle of pills out of her pocket and took two without water.

'Three years.'

'Did you know Professor Ruttershields well?'

'Yes, quite well.'

'Did you get on with him?'

'No. He only kept me on because he said I was such a good cook.'

Florry, who was a hypochondriac as well as an oddball, instinctively felt her pulse and noticed it was racing.

'Did you hate him?' asked Massey.

'No, I just disliked him. He was a right patronising bastard. He was a distinguished man in his field, but he was rude, arrogant and sarcastic. He was one of them nerds who thought he was God.

'For a gentleman, which he clearly thought he was, he didn't half eff and blind at me. I wouldn't have thought a man of his background could be like that.'

'What sort of things did he say to you?'

'One morning at breakfast, he stormed into the

24

kitchen and shouted, "There's too much salt in the scrambled eggs, you silly bitch!" '

Shortly after his separation from his wife, Ruttershields had gone to Russia accompanied by his cook who happened to speak Russian. They stayed in adjacent rooms in the Rossia Hotel in Moscow.

Because of the way Ruttershields had treated her, Florry became emotionally involved with Communism and even joined the Party.

Ruttershields left her alone in the evenings so that he could drink to excess in the bar of the hotel.

Florry was such a starry-eyed Communist that she automatically regarded all Russians as gods, even if the hostile and suspicious behaviour of the Muscovites proved otherwise. In a pathetic sort of way, she would suck up to everyone she met, yearning for approval and longing to be recognised as a model disciple of Marx.

Mrs Ruttershields had advised her not to accept invitations from strangers to parties, because of the way foreigners' drinks were spiked during the cold war.

Florry was walking down the corridor at 11.55 p.m. on her way to her room. A young Russian approached her and invited her to a drinks party. She replied in Russian with excessive reverence.

'It's now five to twelve and if I don't get back to my room by twelve o'clock, I'll miss hearing your glorious National Anthem being played on the radio.'

The man backed slowly out of her presence, astounded.

Ruttershields, by coincidence, was going to his own room at the same time.

'Jesus, Florry, what the hell did you say to that man? He looked as if he were about to expire.'

Florry told him.

'Oh, I do wish you'd stop being so blasted eccentric!' he snarled.

Massey continued the interrogation. Florry became more relaxed. It was the state of public lavatories in East European countries which made her shed her faith in Communism. She veered from the matter in hand.

'In his manifesto, Lenin said, "We will build gold latrines for the workers." I happened to go to the lavatory in East Berlin and I expected it to be made of gold. This was not the case. The lavatory was absolutely filthy and when I pulled the chain, the ballcock came away in my hand and the tank crashed to the floor.'

Massey became exasperated.

'I'm not conducting this enquiry to hear about lavatories!' he rasped. 'Do you know whether you were the only person to dislike him?'

Florry thought a while.

'None of the cooks before me could stand him. They all pissed off in droves.'

'How did he get on with his family?'

'Mrs Ruttershields could never forgive him for being gay. I think the only people who were fond of him were his son and daughter. He was a really mean man. Do you know he wouldn't even let me have time off to take my driving test.'

'Did you kill him, Florry?' asked Massey suddenly.

'Nah! He wouldn't have been worth the space in

the mortuary. Besides, I wouldn't want to be slung into Holloway with a bloody great colony of lesbians crawling into me!'

Massey cleared his throat. An instinct told him that this woman couldn't possibly have killed Ruttershields.

The next person to be questioned was a doctor who had given his name and address in the Royal Society of Medicine after Ruttershields's body had been found. He was a genial, Scottish physician called Dr McInley who was a Consultant in Rheumatology.

Dr McInley was less popular with other members of his profession but his secretaries adulated him because of his inordinate kindness towards them.

He was also a very jolly man. He was full of jokes and for reasons no one understood, he walked down the corridors of the Charing Cross Hospital where he did his NHS work, whistling Red marching songs.

He gave his staff generous presents at Christmas, rarely ticked them off and gave them credit when credit was due.

Dr McInley ran a farm in Hertfordshire at weekends and owned a fishing boat in Scotland which he used on holidays.

'Dr McInley, can you tell me anything about Frederick Ruttershields?' asked Massey.

The doctor ran his hands through his hair.

'I can't say I know an awful lot about him. He was a bit off my beat. What I hated most of all was being mistaken for him. He wasn't a very popular man.'

'In what way?'

'He was a loner, a very antisocial man. He never attended any functions and never joined in anything. Also, he was a very rude man. His secretaries were always in tears, but he did get on extremely well with his personal assistant, Ruth Shenton, who was admitted to hospital with shock when he died.'

Massey tapped his pen on his lower lip, a habit which was intensely irritating to others.

'What was he hiding that made other doctors envious of him?'

'I have absolutely no idea. I told you he wasn't on my beat. He certainly didn't possess anything of interest to me. I'm not interested in what some quack has in his possession. It could be a sex aid for all I care.'

'Did you like him personally?'

'Not particularly. I thought his personal habits left much to be desired. He left disgusting messes in lavatories and the cleaners were always complaining about it. He also had very bad manners getting in and out of lifts. Once, an elderly lady was waiting outside the lift at the Royal Society of Medicine and although he saw her, he didn't have the patience to wait. He just pushed the button to go up.'

Massey was beginning to find the number of witnesses who disliked Ruttershields tedious and misleading. He was frustrated by the task of interviewing many others, all of whom appeared to dislike him on account of his abrasive manner, making it more and more arduous to find the killer.

* * *

Joss Dexter, F.R.C.S. was a plastic surgeon. He was a cheeky, prankish, rather roguish man with a girl always on his arm and a beaming smile never from his lips. He was firmly committed to his trade and lapped up the gratitude and praise of hundreds of women whom he transformed from the ravages of age to youth.

Dexter was one of the doctors in the Royal Society of Medicine at the time of Ruttershields's death. He had thick, blond hair parted in the centre, large, liquid-grey eyes and a fetching, aquiline profile. The adoration poured on him by women made him arrogant and cocky, but he was kind to his underlings, many of whom were women, who made themselves glamorous in order to impress him.

Massey returned to the reception area at the Royal Society of Medicine. It was the turn of Muriel Thomas, a skinny, bad-tempered woman, to take charge.

'Detective Inspector Massey, Scotland Yard,' rasped Massey. 'I'm dealing with the Ruttershields murder enquiry. I've come to speak to the plastic surgeon, Joss Dexter.'

Muriel disliked Massey's tone and was deliberately slow in looking through her diary.

She turned her pasty face, like that of an ex-con, to Massey.

'Mr Dexter's operating in the London Clinic this afternoon.'

'What floor and what theatre?'

'Did you win a scholarship to the charm school you attended?' asked Muriel.

'Cut the crap, sister! I asked what floor and what theatre?'

'Third floor. Theatre H.'

Massey turned to go without thanking her.

'There are such words as "thank you", Inspector.'

The patient lying on Dexter's table was a 50-year-old woman who had taken no care over the years to maintain her youth. There were lines on her forehead, sagging bags under her eyes and furrowed lines on either side of her mouth.

While operating, Dexter sang a catchy, popular song called *Money, Money, Money* under his breath.

He made an incision at the patient's hairline across her face and stretched the skin until it was taut in his hands. He scraped the fat away from under the layer of skin and stretched it like a piece of elastic, pulling it behind the hairline and stitching it. As he stitched it, he sang *From crone to queen, from crone to queen*, to the tune of the 'Habanera' aria from *Carmen*.

Suddenly, the door to the operating theatre was kicked open by Massey. Dexter abandoned his instruments and rushed forward to challenge him.

'You've no business crashing into a sterilised operating theatre when you're not scrubbed up. Get out or I'll call the police.'

'Sir, we are the police.'

Massey flashed his card.

'In that case, you'll have the decency and respect for hygiene to wait outside. I've never encountered such outrageous behaviour in the whole of my career.'

Once he had finished the resurrection of his patient's youth and managed to pinch a few nurses' behinds, Dexter removed his overalls and went out to see Massey.

'Do you know you could be stripped of your rank for barging into an operating theatre like that?'

Massey had little, if any, respect for the medical profession and was infuriated by this seemingly bureaucratic surgeon.

'Mr Joss Dexter?'

'Mr Joss Dexter, F.R.C.S. What do you want?'

'I'd like you to answer a few questions. Is there an office we could go into?'

'Yes. What's all this in aid of? I've got another woman's face to do in half an hour so you'd better make it snappy.'

'I've come about the Ruttershields murder in the Royal Society of Medicine. You were among the people in the building at the time. You gave your name and address.'

'So what if I did? So did hundreds of others.'

Massey tapped his lower lip with his pen which infuriated most people he came in contact with, including Dexter.

'You must understand, I have to question you to elminate you from our enquines, just as I have to question the others.'

Dexter and Massey sat down in an unoccupied secretary's office.

'Your full name, please.'

'Joshua David Edward Dexter.'

'Date of birth?'

'8th July 1952. I told you this already in the Royal Society of Medicine. I don't understand why you have to ask again.'

'How well did you know Professor Ruttershields?' asked Massey, ignoring Dexter's remark.

'I didn't know him at all,' said Dexter, fidgeting in his chair because he didn't want to be late for his operation.

'You mean you didn't know Ruttershields?'

Dexter crossed and uncrossed his legs.

'I've just said I didn't! What's the matter with you? Are you deaf?'

'Don't get cocky with me. Even a plastic surgeon isn't exempt from arrest.'

'The only thing I know of Ruttershields is his name. I don't even know his specialty. All I know is that he's been murdered. I know his name because I had to look up the name Dr Rutter in the medical directory. I happened to see the name Ruttershields underneath it. I thought it was a strange name but I've never met the man. I have to be in another theatre in ten minutes. I'd be obliged if you'd leave me now. I've got to get scrubbed up yet again.'

Massey got up.

'All right, Mr Dexter. I have your address and might need to call on you again.'

'You do that. Any idea when, so that I can cross off the days in anticipation?'

Massey turned round slowly and menacingly to face Dexter.

'I wouldn't get too cheeky if I were you, my friend. Your arrogance might land you behind bars.'

32

'Piss off, guv,' muttered Dexter.

Dexter was almost as eccentric as the Ruttershields's cook, Florry Shanks. He had an elder brother called Joe and was born and bred in central London. He was brought up in Barton Street, Westminster, and was lulled to sleep each night by the comforting chimes of Big Ben.

His greatest love was for his mother, Sylvia, a beautiful woman with blonde hair who doted on her youngest son and denied him nothing. He was wild and unruly at the best of times but when his mother died, his grief, instead of mellowing him, caused him to be uncontrollable.

His father, Jeff Dexter, was an orchestral conductor and a man of considerable wealth. It was evident that Joss had inherited his father's musicianship and Jeff arranged for him to have piano lessons during school holidays as a form of therapy to control his unstable behaviour.

Sylvia's death had brought the Dexter family closer together and Jeff never administered corporal punishment to Joss. Instead, he would talk to him in an effort to find out why he was unable to control his behaviour.

One of the young Dexter's least popular pastimes was throwing stones at vehicles travelling along the Embankment. The target he chose on this occasion was an immaculately clean, bottle-green Jaguar, driven by a flashy-looking, lingerie salesman with slicked back, black hair.

When the stone hit the left hand side of his car, the salesman pulled in to the kerb and leapt out. He went straight for Joss.

'Did you throw that stone, you little bastard?'

Joss began to giggle hysterically.

'Where do you live? I'm taking you straight home to your parents.'

Joss ran off. The salesman pursued him all the way to his house. The door was opened by Jeff who was astonished to see the livid salesman holding Joss by the collar.

'Who are you? Kindly take your hands off my son.'

'Your son has just thrown a stone at my car. I'm going to have to get the whole panel replaced.'

Jeff looked aghast. He was still grieving heavily for his wife.

'Is this true, Joss?'

'Yes. I was only having a bit of fun.'

Jeff turned to the salesman.

'Please accept my most sincere apologies. My wife died recently and her death has had a terrible effect on my son.'

The salesman shifted nervously from one foot to the other.

'I'm sorry to hear that, but my car's pretty badly dented.'

'You'd better come in. Would you mind telling me how much you estimate the damage to be?'

'It will cost at least £100 to repair the panel.'

Jeff took his cheque book from his wallet in his inside pocket.

'Who do I make it out to?'

'Desmond Gilroy, sir.'

Jeff tore the cheque from his cheque book and handed it to Gilroy.

'Thank you, sir. I'm so sorry about your wife. I'll be on my way.'

When Gilroy had gone, Jeff called Joss into his study. Both man and boy remained standing.

'I'm not very pleased with you, Joshua, to say the least. Why did you throw that stone?'

'I was angry.'

'What, with the driver? What had he done to make you angry?'

'I'm angry because Mummy's died.'

Jeff poured himself some whisky.

'Come and sit down beside me, Joss.

'One thing you must understand in life is that no one can live for ever. There must come a time when someone dear to us has to die and for that person's sake, we must carry on. Moral courage is a far finer thing than physical courage. Your mother would be horrified if you habitually threw stones at passing cars to show your grief. You could have caused a fatal accident. Don't ever do anything like that again.'

'No, I won't. I'm very sorry.'

Joss's guilt was short-lived. He had taken a dislike to the gardener who tended the small garden at the back of the house. Joss dug a hole in the garden path and covered it with sticks and branches. The gardener fell into the hole and broke his leg.

Not long after that, Joss was sent to Harrow.

During his late adolescence, marked wildness and eccentricity continued to pervade his personality. He had an irrational hatred of golf club secretaries and even when they failed to provoke him, he would imagine he was being slighted by them and throw himself into violent arguments with them.

The main cause of his animosity towards golf club secretaries was the memory of being addressed by one of them as 'sonny' at the age of ten, when he had made a particular effort to look older.

On one occasion, aged 20, he went to a golf course accompanied by Jeff and Joe. It began to rain shortly after their game had started and Joss stormed into the secretary's office.

'It's raining and I want a refund of my green fee.'

The secretary, who was a stout, bald man and who failed to look Joss in the eye, gaped vacantly into space.

'The club is not responsible for the weather, sir. We cannot give you a refund of your green fee.'

'Look me in the eye when you're talking to me, man!'

'I would appreciate it if you would go away.'

Jeff, who was in a good mood because he was playing better than Joe, wondered where Joss had gone. He returned to the club at the end of the game and was astounded to hear him bellowing at the secretary.

'Would you please take your son off the premises, Mr Dexter. He's being a dreadful nuisance.'

Jeff decided to take his boys to another golf club the following weekend, for fear of being embarrassed further by his wayward son.

Before the game, Joss went to the bathroom. The club secretary, who coincidentally, bore a close resemblance to the previous secretary, went in behind him as Joss held the door open. The secretary went straight to the urinal and saw Joss standing just behind him.

'I held the door open for you, my good man,' said Joss, 'and I didn't hear so much as a blessed murmur!'

The three men went out onto the golf course which was graced with idyllic countryside.

Jeff and Joe used the men's tee but Joss preferred to use the women's tee. He took a swing and sent the ball about 100 yards. He was unaware that the secretary was standing immediately behind him.

'Excuse me, sir, are you a woman?'

'Yes, as a matter of fact I am,' said Joss.

'I'm afraid I must ask you to go to the men's tee.'

'Why should I? We're not living in Hitler's Germany.'

The secretary had never been thus addressed in his life.

'Sir, I suggest you move.'

'I won't,' said Joss.

'You will have to. You are violating the rules of the club.'

Joss raised his golf club as if to strike the secretary.

'Piss off, you oaf!' he shouted.

Joss also went through a phase of telling anyone who happened to cross his path that he was a magistrate. While he was doing his A levels, he went into a pub which had a notice saying 'Good hot food always available' outside.

He went straight in and asked where the food was.

'Sorry, sir, there's no food today.'

'This is nothing short of disgraceful!' shouted Joss.

'You've got a notice outside saying you serve meals and you don't. I am a magistrate. I sit on the Basingstoke Assizes every Friday afternoon and I note you to be in blatant contravention of the Trades Descriptions Act of 1964.' (The date was invented.)

The publican whitened and rushed downstairs to the kitchen.

'Which do you require, sir, egg sandwiches or cottage pie?'

'Cottage pie, please.'

Within ten minutes, a hot cottage pie was produced.

'I apologise for the delay, sir. It's just that we're a bit short-staffed today. Next time you pass by, I can assure you it won't happen.'

'Kindly see that it doesn't.'

Joss was driving too close to the vehicle in front of him on a deserted, country lane, trying to overtake. The driver in front slowed down abruptly, seeing a squirrel on the road. Joss crashed into the back of him and started ticking the man off before he had a chance to speak.

'I am a magistrate. I sit on the Basingstoke Assizes on Friday afternoons. It was not I who ran into the back of you. It was you who reversed into the front of me. I'll see you get a stiff sentence when you come before my bench.'

The other driver was struck dumb. His car was not insured.

'What do I owe you, sir?'

'It's not a bad knock. Make it £75.'

'I'll write you out a cheque for that amount straight away, sir.'

Before settling down at medical school, Joss did odd jobs here and there to satisfy his father's puritanical work ethic. He moved to Plymouth which he hated, partly because it was so far away from London and mainly because he considered it such a supremely grey, depressing city.

He managed to find a job in a ferry company which delegated mundane tasks such as pulling ropes. His bos'un felt he was not putting his back into his work and fired him.

This was an occasion when he was unable to say that he was a magistrate, so one night, he untied the ropes of three ferries and set them all adrift.

His career as a medical student was more successful. He passed all his exams with distinction and started off as a GP before going into general surgery and from there to plastic surgery.

Hadrian Tremlitt, a consultant psychiatrist, was among the people present at the time of the murder, although he appeared too much out of touch with reality to realise Ruttershields himself was the victim. Coincidentally, he had treated Tiger Jenkins, Ruttershields's lover, in an abortive attempt to get him off heroin. Tremlitt was a tall, slender man with brown hair in a short back and sides. He was a homosexual who had had an ongoing, steamy affair with Jenkins. He had a resonant, upper-class accent.

Massey was ushered into his Harley Street consulting rooms accompanied by Bush. Tremlitt, who was a manic depressive, was going through a manic phase at the time. He was strutting up and down in his dingy, damp consulting room, brandishing a swagger-stick.

'Come on boys, come on in! Take a look at the invitations on my mantelpiece. I've been invited to the Queen's Garden Party.'

'Cut your social arrangements,' said Massey. 'This is a murder enquiry.'

Tremlitt continued to flounce up and down the room.

'A murder enquiry? How absolutely thrilling! I suspect Professor Jones in the pantry with the spanner.'

Massey became more and more impatient but failed to interrupt Tremlitt. Bush laughed into his hand.

'Do you know what I tell them if I think they're clinic meat? I come into the consulting room and say, "Absolutely strapping stuff, sex, hey, what! Do you know what I do just afterwards? I bung my stinking carcase out of bed, wipe the spunk off my hampton and crash into a bath. After that, I go for a spiffing good run round the block. Then I burn up to the kitchen where I make four socking great crumpets, all of them absolutely squelching with butter. Then I bowl upstairs and start all over again, what!"'

Massey was fidgeting throughout as Bush continued to giggle.

'Do spare us the details of your sex life, Dr Tremlitt. How well did you know Frederick Ruttershields?'

'Frederick Ruttershields? I can't say I like him much. I found him having it off in a lavatory at the Royal Society of Medicine with Tiger Jenkins, if you please, screaming the bloody building down. I am and always have been in love with Tiger Jenkins and Ruttershields went and nicked him, blast it!'

Massey drilled his eyes into those of Tremlitt.

'Did that provoke you into killing him?'

'Killing him? Killing him? I didn't even know he was dead.'

'Of course you knew. You gave your name and address when he was found.'

Tremlitt used his swagger-stick to scratch his back.

'I knew there'd been an act of violence but I had no idea that Frederick Ruttershields had been murdered. Quite frankly, I'm not sorry. He was such an obnoxious man.'

'But you didn't kill him?'

'No. One just doesn't go round killing those one dislikes. Were that the case, there'd be no room in the graveyards and the crematoria would run out of coal.'

'Dr Tremlitt,' said Massey, 'I will tolerate no more of your buffoonery. Would you please accompany us to the police station, pending further investigations.'

'What the blazes for? I'm innocent of this man's murder. Just because I didn't like him, it doesn't mean I wanted to kill him.'

'Come on, Dr Tremlitt,' said Bush. 'We have to eliminate you from our enquiries.'

Dr Tremlitt was kept at the police station for two hours but was not charged.

Massey and Bush were at the station drinking tea in the tiny, dirty room they referred to, if euphemistically, as the 'canteen'.

Bush was in awe of Massey because of their differences in rank and waited for him to speak first.

'What did you make of Tremlitt?' asked Massey.

'I thought he was bloomin' bonkers. A fruitcake like him would make a dangerous, mental patient look like the Prime Minister.'

Massey smiled.

'One has to be certified insane before one is allowed to practise as a psychiatrist,' he said.

Bush let out a sycophantic guffaw. Massey passed him the visiting card bearing the name and address of the next suspect, Douglas Ferdinand Interkos.

Douglas Interkos was a mild-voiced funeral director, who lived over his shop in Hampstead High Street. He had a Greek father and an English mother. Massey and Bush were puzzled by the fact that he specialised in funeral direction and not medicine.

The time was 7.00 p.m. A sign in his shop window stated: *Douglas Interkos – Funeral Director and Monumental Mason.* Massey rang the bell. Within a minute, a grotesquely fat, red-haired woman, with nothing to hide her nakedness but a skimpy towel, appeared at the door.

She spoke with a strong, Yorkshire accent and had a trenchant, penetrating voice.

'Is one of the hearses parked on a double yellow line?'

'Don't mess about,' barked Massey. 'We wish to speak to Mr Douglas Ferdinand Intercourse.'

'He's having his rest at the moment. I don't want

to wake him. He's had the most ghastly day. The parson attending to one of his funerals gave himself a heroin injection by the graveside and an incident like that is terrible for the firm.'

'I'm not interested in anecdotes!' rasped Massey. 'We'd appreciate it if you'd ask your husband to come down.'

Mrs Interkos felt intimidated by Massey and wished he had come to make arrangements for his own burial rather than rant at her when she hadn't broken the law.

Within ten minutes, Douglas Interkos shuffled downstairs in a quilted dressing gown and carpet slippers.

'Are you Douglas Intercourse?'

Interkos was particularly abrupt because he had been roused prematurely from sleep.

'My name is Douglas Interkos, not Douglas Intercourse. I find you extremely rude. You have no business speaking to my wife like that. We're not living under a dictatorship.'

'I don't recall suggesting we were,' said Massey. 'We came here because we took your name and address on the morning of Professor Frederick Ruttershields's murder on 3rd September at the Royal Society of Medicine.'

Interkos looked baffled.

'Why don't you come in? I don't want the neighbours to see the police standing on my doorstep, I've had a bad enough day already.'

Massey failed yet again to contain his impatience. He wished the police were allowed to use truncheons as a matter of course, no matter how harmless the people answering their questions were.

'I don't care about your bad day! We're coming in.'

Interkos led them through a dour, windowless chapel of rest and into another windowless waiting room.

'This is a pretty gloomy joint,' said Massey.

'That's because we deal with the dead. We are not an upmarket travel bureau,' replied Interkos.

In the thin, pinkish light of the waiting room it first dawned on Massey what Interkos looked like. He was about six foot tall, his black hair was streaked with white and he wore a goatee beard. His appearance was by no means undistinguished. Massey forced himself to treat him with respect.

'Do you mind if I ask you what you were doing at the Royal Society of Medicine on 3rd September? It's hardly a funeral director's beat.'

Interkos, who was sitting on a hard-backed sofa by his wife's side, leant forward and stroked his beard.

'I'd been in the library the night before. I went to consult a book on forensic medicine. The book was entitled *Revolutionary Embalming Techniques* and according to a review in the *Lancet*, which I subscribe to, despite the fact that I am not a doctor, there is a new embalming fluid which is said to be more long-lasting than formaldehyde.'

Massey was temporarily struck dumb. Interkos's voice was quiet, gentle and unaggressive. He regretted his hostile manner earlier and felt ashamed. Eventually, he composed himself.

'Were you in the library all night?'

'No. It was so hot in there that I fainted. I felt really shaken by it and eventually I lay down in a corridor and fell asleep.'

Massey peered into Interkos's eyes but remained uncharacteristically courteous.

'Might I ask if your business is proceeding satisfactorily? Here we are, in the heat of a recession, but your profits must be greater than most, since no recession can stop people dying.'

Interkos fidgeted in his chair and lit a king-sized cigarette.

'Want one? It's good for business.'

'No,' said Massey curtly. 'I can't stand the smell of tobacco.'

Interkos suddenly got irritated.

'You seem to think that individuals like us are wealthy just because people die. I can't begin to tell you what a stupid and irresponsible remark you've just made. Most people can't afford my funerals. They often bury their dead in their gardens.

'Then there is the problem with cancer specialists and other specialists who prolong life beyond its natural span. Those are the people who ruin my trade, not to mention batty parsons who inject themselves with heroin by the graveside.'

Massey sat forward in his chair.

'You seem to have a grievance against parties who postpone death.'

'What undertaker wouldn't?' asked Interkos, his voice raised in anger.

'I'm afraid you will have to accompany us to the police station; we have further enquiries to make.'

*   *   *

Professor Frederick Ruttershields was brought up in a Queen Anne house near the Yorkshire Moors. The family owned another house in Eaton Square, London. His father, Miles Ruttershields, was a general and played little part in the upbringing of his son.

As Frederick grew from a toddler to a child, Miles would only contact him to chastise him both physically and verbally.

Frederick's mother's name was Anne. She was a distinguished, auburn-haired woman who had even less contact with him, but on the few occasions that she saw him, she rang the servants' bell and had him brought down to the drawing room, dressed up as if for a party.

'Do take your bricks over to another part of the room, Freddie,' his mother would say, while she sat by the fire and read a book. At least she could see her son in the distance although she never played with him or took him on her knee.

Frederick was an only child and his birth had been an accident. Miles, his father, was adamant that he wanted no children in his house and when Frederick came down after tea he would retire to another room to look at maps and anything else that took his fancy.

'Why don't you ever talk to me, Mother?' asked Frederick on one occasion.

'But Freddie, I can see you. I can watch you. There's no need for me to say anything to you.'

His mother owned a small, yapping Basset called

Pop-Eye. Its grating barks alone were enough to antagonise Frederick. His mother never stopped caressing it and talking to it.

'Whom do you love most, Mother, Pop-Eye or me?'

'You are a silly boy. I love you most.'

'Then why do you always have Pop-Eye on your knee and ignore me?'

Mrs Ruttershields kissed Pop-Eye and laid him gently on the floor.

'Of course, I love you more than Pop-Eye.'

'I don't think you do. You shouldn't have had me if you're not going to take any notice of me.'

Mrs Ruttershields considered her son's behaviour impertinent.

'You are a rude brat,' she said. 'I think we ought to wait for your father to come home.'

Miles Ruttershields later strode into the drawing room, wearing only socks because his boots were muddy.

Anne immediately complained about Frederick.

'Miles, dear, I can't tolerate that boy coming down to the drawing room any longer. He was so rude this evening,' she said within Frederick's hearing.

'Was the little blighter, now? What did he say?'

'He said in so many words, that I should never have brought him into the world if I were going to ignore him.'

Miles turned to Frederick who was kneeling, stoking the log fire.

'Is this true, Frederick?'

'Yes, and I meant it. Mother only sees me when

she sends for me, and then all she does is talk to Pop-Eye.'

Miles flew into a thunderous rage.

'You'd better come to the library, Frederick. You and I have something to discuss.'

Frederick followed his father into the library, expecting a verbal reprimand. Miles opened the drawer and pulled out a menacing-looking cane which made a whirring noise as he swept it through the air as a ploy to terrify the boy.

'Bend over against the table and take off your shorts.'

Frederick obeyed. His father lashed him like a madman, causing livid welts to appear on his behind.

'You can get up now,' said his father.

Frederick struggled to get into an upright position.

'You're supposed to say "thank you" after a beating.' He extended his hand.

'Thank you, Father,' the boy muttered.

The following day, Frederick overheard his parents talking.

'Personally, I am to blame,' his mother said. 'We both know Frederick was an accident because I was too tired to put my cap in straight.'

'You weren't tired. You were bone idle. If you'd taken the trouble to cover it with jelly and put it in straight, we would never have had Frederick on our hands.'

Frederick swiftly opened the door.

'I overheard all that,' he said. 'I wish you could get me adopted since you obviously care so little for me.'

Miles and Anne couldn't stand rows.

The next morning at breakfast, Anne was alone at the table. Miles joined her.

'Anne, I've got the perfect solution.'

Anne continued to sip her coffee.

'Well, what is the solution?'

'Send him away to Sunningdale of course. We put him down for Eton when he was born, just to get him off our hands, and when the term ends, we can fit him into a holiday home where they send orphans.'

Anne crossed and uncrossed her legs.

'Oh, darling, how perfectly divine! I couldn't have come up with a better idea myself.'

Once at Eton, Frederick was aloof, withdrawn and subdued, but he came to welcome the permanent presence of others around him, to alleviate the loneliness and gloom his parents had caused him.

At first, he felt no need to speak to his fellow pupils. Their presence around him was enough. When he recovered from his shyness, he built up a circle of friends and an equally large circle of enemies, who resented his peculiar behaviour, manifesting itself in his lying permanently on his back on his fold-up bed, to which he would retire like an animal in hibernation.

A boy called Mike Curtis had taken an instant liking to Frederick, because he had scrambled onto his desk at the end of a Latin lesson and sung *By the Light of Burning Martyrs* in an attempt to attract attention to himself without establishing a speaking relationship.

Curtis came into Frederick's room.

'Come on Rutters, let's go out into the town after class and get drunk. I've got a bottle of gin in my suitcase.'

'Socking good idea, what?' replied Frederick, desperately trying to overdo an upper-class accent to gain social acceptance.

Curtis and Frederick left the school compound and sat by the river which was draped with weeping willows. The boys passed the bottle to each other until they were pie-eyed. Frederick told the story of his life for the first time.

'I say, Fred, that all sounds a bit rough. But let me advise you as one friend to another – try to think of the future, not the past. If you don't, you'll drive yourself mad.'

Curtis's kind words caused Frederick to burst into tears. He rested his head on Curtis's shoulder.

Suddenly, Frederick felt a strange thrill as he once thought he would feel were his companion a woman. The two boys kissed and thereafter shared the same bed each night.

Another person Frederick felt emotionally and sexually drawn towards was the house matron, Miss Birch. Miss Birch had long, bleached, peroxide hair, coiled modestly into a bun which accentuated her plump figure and made her look the epitome of Diana Dors. She was 35 years of age.

Miss Birch's face was completely unlined, almost unnaturally so for a woman of her age. Her eyes were Caribbean blue and her overall a bit too low cut to be up to an Etonian matron's standards.

Frederick developed a crush on her and yearned for an occasion to sit next to her, if only to gaze at her pure, untarnished face. He almost fainted when she first spoke to him.

'Now, come along, Ruttershields, dear, if you don't eat up your greens you're not going to grow into a strong man.'

Frederick's heart was beating so fast that he was terrified Miss Birch would hear it.

'I'm sorry, Miss Birch. It won't happen again.'

'See that it doesn't. We can't have you shirking your duties at the wall game* this afternoon.'

'No, Miss Birch.'

The boys ate in a rectangular dining room with long tables. Frederick and Curtis were sitting on either side of Miss Birch, who sat at the head of the table, serenely staring into space. She laid her hand on her chest, accentuating her revealing overall with a generalised air of mystery.

Apart from Frederick, the boys on each side of the table found her demure gestures comical. Collectively, they embarked on a programme of disguised and undiagnosable insolence by the bombardment of mechanical overtures.

'Nice day, Miss Birch.'

She continued to lay her hand on her cleavage and smiled enigmatically.

---

* The wall game: A game played exclusively at Eton, involving the use of a wall.

51

'Spring greens, Miss Birch?'

'Salt, Miss Birch?'

'No, thank you.'

'Pepper, Miss Birch?'

'No, thank you.'

'It's dead man's leg today, Miss Birch.'

'Do you need Worcester sauce, Miss Birch?'

'No, thank you.'

'It's the wall game this afternoon, Miss Birch.'

Frederick, who had gazed throughout at Miss Birch's youthful, lineless face, felt the impertinence of his colleagues had exceeded the bounds of decency.

'Miss Birch?'

'Yes, Ruttershields?'

Frederick lowered his head.

'I apologise for all of them, Miss Birch.'

It was not long afterwards that Miss Birch was jilted by her fiancé who fell for another woman. Her fiancé served in the Welsh Guards and her rival had a penchant for men in uniforms. She threw herself at the Welsh Guard with such manic enthusiasm that he was overtly flattered and had already become bored with Miss Birch and her silent, shy temperament.

The manner in which the Guard dismissed Miss Birch, who had chosen a wedding dress with a plunging neckline, was terse.

He pushed a typewritten letter under her door.

Dear Thelma,

Although I was keen on you, I no longer find you lush or stimulating. You hardly ever speak and your performance between the sheets leaves much to be desired.

In short, I have found someone else.
I want our engagement terminated.

Sincerely,
David

Within a year, Miss Birch aged rapidly and looked ten years older. Her face showed deep furrows on each side of her mouth. Her blue eyes, which had lost their allure, had unsightly bags beneath them. Her forehead was lined and even her delicate, slender hands bore the marks and wrinkles of age. In addition, it was known that she had incurable cancer.

Frederick approached Mike Curtis in the quadrangle of the school and took him aside.

'I've made up my mind what I want to do when I leave here.'

'I say. Do tell.'

'I'm going into medicine and once I've qualified, I'm going to prevent beautiful women getting old like poor Miss Birch and I'm going to pioneer a revolutionary cure for cancer.'

'So you're going to be a plastic surgeon.'

'No, but I'd like to know how to rejuvenate a face without anything as drastic as surgery, and find a form of preventive medicine to limit disease and in particular cancer.'

'How can you give a woman back her youth without operating and limit cancer once it's spread?' asked Curtis.

'I'm devoting my life to inventing something, by injection if possible.'

'You must mean collagen injections. They've already been invented.'

'I'm not referring to those,' said Frederick. 'I'm going to find something else. I'm also going to find a way of prolonging life. I have a vision of 120 being the age of retirement and of people living quite comfortably to be 150.'

'You're raving mad,' said Curtis, spitting a grape pip on to one of the paving stones of the quadrangle.

'That's what you think. People thought Galileo was mad when he discovered the theory of falling objects.'

Frederick went to medical school in a central London hospital after leaving Eton. His years of apprenticeship, followed by his eventual qualification as a doctor, were uneventful. He was not overtly sociable and was seen by those who knew him, as a loner.

He met his wife, Sheila, an equally quiet and reserved woman during a lecture on sexually transmitted diseases and was attracted by her mane of black hair, discretely streaked with red. She too, was training to be a doctor.

She accepted his invitation to dinner at a French restaurant in Soho. Throughout the meal they talked entirely about medicine, as if neither of them had any interests outside the field.

Sheila was impressed by Frederick's plans to prevent cancer and halt the ageing process and admired his persistence and single-mindedness.

'How are you going to set about doing that when both cancer and ageing have defeated the medical profession for centuries?'

'Have you not heard about ozone?' asked Frederick.

Sheila was embarrassed by her ignorance.

'I've heard about the ozone layer in the sky but I don't see what that's got to do with your plans.'

Frederick crammed three mussels into his mouth.

'Ozone is a substance that lives all around us, in plants and trees, for instance. Obviously, that's not enough to prevent ageing and disease. It has to be used in a concentrated form. I've researched the matter in detail and the ozone I plan to inject my patients with comes in the form of liquid, concentrated oxygen. The only place it is used at the moment is Mexico.'

'Where did you get all this information?' asked Sheila.

'From the research I've been doing at the Royal Society of Medicine for the past three months. All I need is a machine from Germany, where they make them without knowing about the benefits of ozone. To get it in its most beneficial form, concentrated oxygen has to be sucked into the machine and converted to liquid and injected into the muscle. It's the equipment itself rather then the substance which is so costly. That's why I'm writing a book about it. Once it's published, other doctors will use the machine and the more widely it's used, the more its cost will go down, so that everybody can afford to be injected regularly. That way, more and more patients will be rejuvenated and immunised against both serious and minor illness. AIDS, too, will be kept at bay by ozone.'

Sheila was finding her pâté too rich. She reached across the table and took two mussels from Frederick's plate.

'Somehow, I don't think you're going to pull this off, Frederick,' she said as she forced open the two shells to get at the mussels.

'Your pessimism is only a sign of your ignorance. I have started to write a book on the subject which will take quite a few years. The purpose of my book is to show to doctors and laymen alike the function of these injections in successfully treating not just cancer and ageing but all other bodily ailments, among which AIDS is one.'*

Frederick was getting so excited by discussing his subject that he had no idea he was shouting.

'Do keep your voice down, Frederick. Surely you don't want the entire restaurant to know your business.'

Frederick continued, this time more quietly.

'There was a case of a man in Mexico who had terminal cancer of the liver. Thirty years ago, he was told he had three months to live. Because of these ozone injections, the man was completely cured. He is still alive.

'There is another case involving an actress who looked seventy at the age of forty-five and who had a morbid fear of face-lifts. She went to Mexico for six months and had ozone injections four times a week. Now, apparently, she doesn't look much older than thirty.'

---

*By courtesy of the late Dr Victor Ratner, author of the unpublished work, *Medicine's Presumptuous Attitude – The Ozone Miracle*.

Frederick had been so carried away talking about his discovery that he failed to notice that Sheila was yawning.

'I don't believe in any of this,' she said with her eyes almost shut.

Suddenly, Frederick realised he was boring her. He had planned to propose marriage to her that evening.

'I'm sorry to have been banging on about my subject,' he said with exaggerated false modesty. 'Do you have any plans for your career?'

Sheila stretched across the table for another of the mussels Frederick had left uneaten. She winced when she put it in her mouth as it was cold.

'I've no great plans the way you have. All I want is to marry, settle down and have children. Once they are grown up, I want to continue in my chosen field of radiotherapy.'

Later that evening, Frederick proposed to her. Within three months they were married.

Frederick continued to write his book and still had not launched it by the time of his death when Marius and Miriam were 18 and eleven.

He had already built up a lucrative practice, treating film stars, members of the Royal family and millionaires. He had become a millionaire himself and because he was so secretive about his book and the therapy it pioneered, other doctors in Harley Street became baffled and did all they could to determine the secret of his trade. While their custom was dwindling, plastic surgeons began to hear about Frederick, who had the power to restore ageing women's faces without surgery.

Once his book neared completion, Frederick planned to launch it in front of his colleagues and national as well as international journalists. He had even organised a band and some singers to sing a catchy, if banal song to the tune of 'Dinah, Dinah, Show Us Your Leg'.

> *Reaper, Reaper lay down your scythe*
> *And use it for tending my land.*
>
> *Plastic surgeon, lay down your knives*
> *And use them for carving my ham.*

He intended to launch his book in the hall of the Royal Society of Medicine at lunchtime on Monday, 3rd September. He had managed to finish reading his proofs by mid-July.

Although he was not always deliberately cruel to Miriam and Marius as they grew up, Frederick was a moody and unpredictable father. There were times when he was affectionate and took them on outings, but he became distanced from them once they had turned from toddlers into children.

Sheila Ruttershields, on the other hand, was a concerned and loving mother while being formidably strict with her children when they were naughty.

Since the children did not get on particularly well,

they pivoted round their mother who was a source of strength and security. Gradually, Sheila began to resent Frederick's worsening attitude and even went so far as to continuously berate him in front of them.

Marius was jealous of Miriam. Miriam suffered from nightmares so her mother moved her from the room she shared with Marius into her own room. Sheila and Frederick had stopped sharing a room after the children were conceived.

Frederick formed a psychological alliance with Marius. They shared a grievance against Sheila for having cast them out, and both developed an unconscious dislike and even hatred towards women.

Miriam craved her father's approval and when it was denied her, she became disturbed and began to walk in her sleep. One night the police found her wandering round an unlocked room in the neighbouring Royal Free Hospital.

Frederick was waiting for her when the police brought her home. Sheila was already asleep.

'Come into my study, Miriam,' said Frederick.

Miriam was still half asleep but did as she was told.

'How dare you wander outside the house once you've been sent to bed!'

'I didn't know what I was doing. I was walking in my sleep.'

'How old are you?'

'Eleven, just turned. You even forgot my birthday.'

'Don't you dare be so impertinent! Bend over.'

Frederick whipped her six times with a flexing riding crop.

In one of many moments of bitterness, he shouted at the terrified girl.

'Don't you ever expect me to treat you any differently from the way my parents treated me! Go upstairs to bed.'

She went to her mother's room and told her what had happened.

'You're a sadist, Frederick,' said Sheila at breakfast in front of the children.

'How do you define "sadist"?' asked Frederick.

'The word "sadism" is derived from a certain Comte de Sade,' began Sheila.

He was not a Comte. He was a Marquis. Now, I'm off to the Royal Society of Medicine.'

'Who with?' shouted Sheila.

'Someone a lot more companionable than you. I won't be back tonight.'

Before he left, the only person he kissed was Marius, which estranged him from his younger sister even more.

Joss Dexter, the plastic surgeon, had been in police custody for nearly three hours. He was exhausted as he had just moved into his new house in Hampstead. He was questioned by two officers in turn and maintained an aura of dumb insolence, his attitude being that he was superior to his questioners.

'Whereabouts were you in the Royal Society of Medicine, early on the morning of 3rd September?' asked Detective Sergeant Bixby.

'I had a room there. I had to prepare some slides first thing that morning.'

'Were you in your room all night?'

Dexter shifted in his chair and ran his fingers through his whitish-blond hair.

'I got up to go to the lavatory at 2.30 a.m. and again at 5.30 a.m.'

'Why did you have to get up twice?'

'I'd been drinking the night before and there was a hell of a lot of liquid in my bladder,' said Dexter with his feet up on a spare chair.

Detective Sergeant Bixby was irritated by Dexter's insolent behaviour and was annoyed because he couldn't levy a charge of dumb impertinence against him.

'What time did you get up, Mr Dexter?'

'Not till everyone was called to the hall on the tannoy.'

'Did you know Frederick Ruttershields?'

'The name's vaguely familiar. I'd never met the fellow. Frankly, he didn't look my type. I can also tell when a man's gay.'

'Mr Dexter,' began Sergeant Bixby, 'did you have any feelings of hatred towards this man?'

Dexter got up in spontaneous frustration and kicked the chair he had been sitting on.

'I've just told you I didn't know him. Why should I have feelings of hatred towards him?'

The two talked exhaustively in circles. Bixby was dismayed that no solution had been reached.

'All right, Mr Dexter, you may go but it is likely that we will call on you again.'

'That's damn decent of you!' snapped Dexter. 'You have wasted no less than two hours of my precious time. My talents are invaluable; it would be an understatement to say yours are not.'

It was some months earlier when Dexter had been sitting with his feet up in his Harley Street office, reading the *Evening Standard* which his secretary always left on his desk.

The telephone rang and he grabbed hold of the receiver.

'Yes? What is it?'

'It's Daddy here. I'm afraid there's been a death in the family.'

'Who's died?'

'Grandad's brother, James.'

Dexter moved his chair closer to the desk because it was a bad line and he had difficulty understanding his father's voice.

'I'm sorry to hear that. Great Uncle James had Alzheimer's disease for over three years. He was ninety-one only recently. He seemed very unhappy in the old people's home. I think we should all regard his death as a merciful release.'

'You're right, Joss. Whenever we went to visit him, he never recognised any of us. He saw us as strangers intruding on him and our visits only made him more anxious. Before his illness, he made a will in which he stated that he wanted to be cremated and have his ashes buried in a cemetery in the Hampstead area where he was born and grew up.'

Joss never liked interruptions when he was working. The conversation with his father was depressing him.

'Leave it to me, Daddy. I'll make all the necessary arrangements.'

'Are you sure?'

'Absolutely sure, but I've got to go now. I have to go and give an old biddy a facelift.'

Dexter took a few days off to arrange his great uncle's funeral. He was irritated by the additional burden of organising a cremation followed by a burial.

He happened to find Douglas Interkos's name in the Yellow Pages.

It was a dour, windy morning and eddies of autumn leaves blew around Dexter's feet. He rang Interkos's bell twice and heard the first bar of the 'Volga Boatman'.

A secretary, dressed in black and white, answered.

'I've come to see Douglas Intercourse.'

'You mean Douglas Interkos. He'll be with you in a moment. Do sit down.'

Dexter was initially shocked by the shabby vulgarity of his surroundings. Dust-covered, marble statues of cherubs stood on an occasional table and an amateur sculpture of the 'Pietà', on a bright green, imitation marble base occupied the other part of the waiting room. Dexter was nervous and began to pace up and down.

'Good morning. I'm Douglas Interkos.'

The man who stood before Dexter was not his vision of a suburban undertaker. His height and distinguished, goatee-bearded face, coupled with his quiet, even humble, verbal delivery, charmed him immediately.

'I've come to make arrangements for a funeral,' said Dexter courteously.

'That is surely confirmed by the fact that you are here,' said Interkos charmingly. 'Won't you come into my office?'

Dexter followed Interkos into his office. He stated what he wanted done but instead of leaving the premises, he stayed behind. The two men drank a bottle of brandy and had a long discussion about philosophy and life.

'You're favoured during this recession,' remarked Dexter. 'Surely no recession can stop people dying.'

Interkos ran his hand through his black, silver-streaked hair.

'I'm afraid you can't be sure of that. So many people are unemployed and can't afford funerals.'

'What do they do with their dead?' asked Dexter.

Interkos laughed.

'Many bury them in their gardens.'

Dexter temporarily reverted to the eccentric and impertinent behaviour of his student days.

'Have you got an overdraft, old boy?'

Interkos, who was occasionally devoid of pomposity, started giggling. He somehow regarded Dexter as an old friend.

'Yes, I have, old boy. Want to know what it is?'

'What?'

'£30,000.'

'That's quite some overdraft!'

'I've taken a liking to you, Mr Dexter.'

'Joss.'

'I was wondering if you'd like to have a game of golf on Saturday afternoon.'

'I don't see why not, Douglas. I'll meet you here at 2.30 and we can go on.'

Interkos was surprised by Dexter's bizarre method of playing golf. He only used one hand to hold the club and whenever his ball was lost in the bushes, he automatically produced another one. Interkos ignored this.

The two men were approaching the green and Interkos's ball went straight onto it without being caught in the bunker.

'It's these bloody cancer specialists who make my overdraft what it is!' exclaimed Interkos.

'I know what you mean. It's these fringe rejuvenation quacks who interfere with my career as a plastic surgeon.'

Dexter putted his ball into the hole.

'I've heard of a certain Frederick Ruttershields,' he said. 'Read a short piece about him in the *Lancet*. He's got some game going. God knows what it is, though. Not only has he set himself up to prolong life so that one can marry at 75, have children at 100, retire at 120 and live until 150. He's also bringing out a book to say how this is done. He claims to be able to make a woman of 80 look 40, without surgery.'

Interkos was so depressed and dismayed that he savagely clutched his club and threw it into the air.

*　*　*

Interkos and Dexter met on subsequent occasions and were mutually concerned about the deterioration of their respective trades. They met frequently, at golf courses, in bars, on country walks and at theatres. The two had become inseparable friends. They were not homosexuals, but, as Dexter put it, they were two men with something in common, namely a homicidal grievance against Frederick Ruttershields.

As their friendship developed, Dexter noted something singular about Interkos. The man had an obsessive preoccupation with illness. Interkos did not appear to welcome illness in the hope that it would lead to death and possibly improve his trade; it was the reverse of this. Regardless of the fact that he had no symptoms, he was so terrified of being taken ill that he would become gloomy for days at a time. At such times, he was too depressed to meet anyone socially.

He attributed his dread of illness to his mother. If he visited the family home on the island of Spetsai with so much as a cold, she would say, 'If you've got a cold, you can't go anywhere near your father. You'll have to eat in another room.'

His father later died of self-neglect after recurrent attacks of pneumonia.

Even when Interkos was well, he nurtured morbid fears of being taken ill, so much so that he asked his overworked doctor to vaccinate him once a week against catarrh and every three months against influenza.

Dexter rang Interkos up one Saturday morning.

'I thought we might have a game of golf today and discuss things during the game.'

Interkos accepted. He was suffering from chest pains that day, and had an unsubstantiated fear that he had heart disease.

He turned up at the golf course wearing a stethoscope.

'What have you got that on for?' shouted Dexter as they teed up.

Interkos clapped his hand to his forehead.

'I haven't told you before, Joss, but I suffer from this crippling fear that I'm going to be taken ill.'

Dexter laid down the club he was going to hit the ball with. He looked exasperated.

'Why?' he asked.

'I've had it all my life. I don't know why. I am too cowardly even to travel by underground. There are so many tramps down there that I'm terrified I'll catch something. Do you know that tuberculosis has mutated three times and there is no longer a cure?'

Dexter took a swing and hit his ball 100 yards.

'That's rubbish,' he said.

Interkos became worried when Dexter failed to keep a golfing appointment the following weekend. He wondered if he had offended Dexter and rang him.

'Hullo, Joss.'

Dexter was in bed with a woman and Interkos had woken him.

'Come on, Douglas, it's 8.30 on a bloody Sunday morning.'

'I was only wondering if we might meet again for golf next week,' suggested Interkos timidly.

'I suppose so, but since we're going to my club, I really must insist that you don't wear that fatuous stethoscope, going ba-boom, ba-boom, ba-boom, ba-boom all over the place.'

'I'm worried about my heart.'

'In that case, worry about it elsewhere and not when you're with me.'

Interkos read all the periodical medical reviews, many of which mentioned the miraculous cures proposed by Ruttershields. The only thing he was able to find out was that once the book was published and the elixir popularised, every doctor in Britain would be using it at a reduced price, thereby ruining his trade.

He began to suffer from insomnia. Because his own interests were paramount to him, he would ring his long-suffering doctor up every 15 minutes of the night.

'I took that crap you gave me to make me sleep and I'm nowhere near asleep. In fact, I feel like running the marathon.'

The time was 1.45 a.m.

Interkos's doctor, Jimmy Cohen, who had been looking after him for two decades, was too kind-hearted to lose his temper.

'When did you take your last Temazepam?' he asked gently.

'Two and a half hours ago. The stuff's useless.'

'May I suggest you take two more?'

'All right, but I bet that won't do me any good either.'

'Try and sleep now.'

Interkos obeyed his doctor. The pills did not work. He lay awake beside his gross-looking wife, and his preoccupation with the dramatic reduction of his profits made him sick with rage.

He rang Dr Cohen again. It was 3.30 a.m.

'I did exactly what you told me to do and I'm still awake.'

Again, Dr Cohen was as patient as ever.

'Did you take your Temazepam?'

'Yes, of course I did!' bellowed Interkos. 'What do I do now?'

Cohen was becoming so exhausted that he spoke scarcely above a whisper.

'Temazepam takes up to an hour to work. Whatever you do, don't take any more. It might kill you.'

Mrs Interkos, who had already been woken twice by Interkos's shouting, gathered her bedclothes together and went to sleep in another room.

'Look, Jimmy, my hour's almost up. I still feel like going for a run.'

Cohen was becoming exasperated by these calls which rained in at regular intervals each night, but because Interkos was an old patient of his, he treated him with disguised respect.

'Are you worried about something?' asked Cohen.

'Worried? Worried? Of course I'm worried! I'm worried about my profits! I'm worried about my liver! I'm worried about my heart! I'm worried about when I'm next going to get a holiday and, on top of that, I'm worried about my friend's dismissive manner on the golf course!'

Cohen had to hold the receiver a yard away from his ear. He assumed his patient was mad and wished he would die of an overdose.

'Mr Interkos,' he explained patiently, 'you must understand that my sleep should be undisturbed so that I can have enough strength to go about my duties. I do wish you'd stop ringing me every fifteen minutes of the night. If you continue to do this, I shan't be able to look after you any more.'

'I'd have no trouble finding other doctors!' shouted Interkos.

Cohen was suddenly stricken with worry.

'Have you got other doctors?'

'Yes, I have.'

'How many, if I might ask?'

'Four, to be precise.'

'In that case, Mr Interkos, for the sake of my own professional safety, I shall have to cross you off my books.'

Interkos and Dexter met again on the golf course the following Saturday. Both were harbouring the same thoughts but neither expressed them. They played in silence for 20 minutes. The silence was eventually broken by Interkos.

'Things are getting so much worse, Joss. My profits have halved and I can't even get to sleep any more.'

Dexter was thrashing about in the undergrowth, trying to find his ball.

'You know what the cause of the trouble is, Douglas. What do you propose to do about it?'

'There's only one thing we can do. That is to kill Ruttershields and find his book and destroy it.'

'That's the first intelligent thing I've ever heard you say, Douglas. We're in this together. Divided we fall.'

Dexter, who had found his ball, hit it about 50 yards. It landed in a bunker.

'Don't think I haven't made any plans,' he said. 'First, I've set up a private dick. Ruttershields is repainting his house. I've sent in a man disguised as a workman. He's a computer expert. All he needs is access to the screen. He's found out that Ruttershields sleeps for two hours in the afternoon. His secretary has been off for over two weeks so I've asked my girlfriend to enrol at the agency he uses. If the private dick finds there's a password and can't break in, my girlfriend will be told the password and will lift everything from the screen and erase the files.'

'But that's just getting it off the screen,' said Interkos.

'When I send my girl in, I'll tell her to ask Ruttershields if he's actually printed anything. If he has, she will ask to see it to check it for errors. Then she will destroy it. Ruttershields will be grossly inconvenienced but because of his doggedness, he will start all over again That's why we will have to get rid of him.'

'Where will the venue be?' asked Interkos.

'In the hall of the Royal Society of Medicine. The

detective has told me he stays there almost every night of the week and is usually accompanied by punk-looking boys whom he refers to as his 'secretaries', on the rare occasions he is questioned.

'The Royal Society of Medicine is unmanned before 9.00 a.m. The detective says Ruttershields has insomnia and often walks round the building in the early morning. I'll pose as a journalist and while I am distracting him, you will smash his brains in with the spiked mace I got from the London Black Museum. My voice sounds much more journalistic and aggressive than yours.'

'Don't you think all this is easier said than done?'

'What murder isn't easier said than done? We've got to get rid of this man. Because of this rejuvenation technique and the proposed postponement of old age, my patients are leaving me in droves. I only managed to do four faces last week when I'm used to doing three a day. If this goes on, I shall end up in a bloody council house.'

(Dexter had deliberately refrained from telling Interkos about his unearned income.)

'How do you propose to get into the Royal Society of Medicine in the small hours of the morning?'

Dexter looked exasperated.

'I have a thing known as a key,' he said.

The two conspirators met again one Saturday afternoon in an uncrowded pub. Interkos felt timid about the plan, but Dexter chided him and said he had it under control.

Jane Everest had been Dexter's girlfriend on and off for two years and was told by her lover to enrol at Office Angels, a medical secretarial employment agency. Dexter provided bogus references.

'What do you do, Jane?' asked the interviewer behind the desk at the agency.

'I can do Word Perfect 5.1 and although I am flexible, I prefer to work for doctors who are doing research.'

'In that case, I think we can definitely help you. I note from your cv that you have worked for doctors all over London. Have you ever met Professor Ruttershields?'

Jane looked down at her clothing before answering. She was wearing a red miniskirt and a white, see-through shirt. Her long black hair was lank and loose.

'No, I've never heard of him.'

After she had passed the tests set for her, the interviewer called Jane to her desk.

'You have done very well, Jane, but I must warn you of two things. First, Professor Ruttershields is rather an old-fashioned gentleman who doesn't care for women in miniskirts. Second, he is very difficult to work for. He's intolerant, particularly of women, and doesn't suffer fools gladly.'

The following Monday morning, Jane rang Ruttershields's bell. She had to wait a while before the door was answered. She had on a brown trouser-suit, a white, polo-neck sweater and brown, suede, lace-up shoes.

A receptionist opened the door.

'Good morning, my name is Jane Everest. I'm from the Office Angels Agency and I have an appointment with Professor Ruttershields.'

The receptionist's manner was almost as unfriendly as her employer's. She jerked her hand upwards.

'His office is on the third floor. You won't find him that easy. He's worked his way through three secretaries in one week alone.'

Jane mounted the stairs silently, anxious to please Dexter by doing what he wanted.

She went to the top floor and advanced towards the only door which was shut. She knocked quietly.

'What do you want?' a man's rasping, upper-class voice called from behind the door.

Jane opened the door and went in.

'How do you do, Professor Ruttershields. My name is Jane Everest and I'm from Office Angels. I gather you sent for me.'

Ruttershields turned round on his swivel chair to face her. The first feature she noticed about him was his piercing eyes. He remained sitting.

'These agencies always get everything wrong. I didn't ask for you till next week.'

Jane gave him a beaming smile.

'What day next week do you need me?'

'Monday. Monday to Friday,' said Ruttershields without getting up.

'Then Monday it shall be,' said Jane.

There was something about Jane which Ruttershields liked. He wished she were a boy with short hair.

'Come back on Monday,' he said.

74

* * *

Ruttershields was in a better mood the following Monday when Jane arrived, as he had just had coffee.

'Coffee, Miss Everest?' he asked.

'Yes, please.'

Once they were settled, Ruttershields handed Jane a tape relating to his miracle cure.

'Do you know how to use Word Perfect 5.1?'

'Yes, but I can't get into the programme.'

Ruttershields smiled.

'That's because you don't know the password.'

'Well, what is the password?'

'TIGER.'

'Do you wish me to print the documents?'

'Yes. One top and one copy.'

'In that case, may I see the top and the copy you have printed before so that all the papers can go together?'

Strangely, Ruttershields was not suspicious. He produced both copies from a drawer.

'I think you are pretty settled now. By lunchtime, I shall expect to find you're up to chapter fifteen.'

Jane turned round and smiled again.

'You can rely on me, Professor Ruttershields.'

Jane waited for Ruttershields to go downstairs to see his patients. Then she pressed the F5 key and rustled up the list of files relating to Ruttershields's book. She erased them one by one, as well as the identical files on the floppy disk next to the computer. She also erased the tape.

She put the original and the copy of the book in her briefcase, and at 12.00 noon she went downstairs where she met Ruttershields in the hall.

'Are you up to chapter fifteen yet, Miss Everest?'

'Yes, I'm well into chapter sixteen. I must go now as I have an appointment.'

Ruttershields watched her as she left the building. There was one thing she didn't know – he had his own handwritten manuscript in his possession, as well as a spare, floppy disc in his safe.

Jane waited until they were in bed before handing the original and copy to Dexter. At first, he was overjoyed.

'You did it that easily? You're a hell of a girl!'

'I know,' said Jane. 'Do I get my reward?'

'This wasn't a business deal. You're getting nothing!' said Dexter. 'Besides, I'm exhausted.'

Dexter decided not to let her know about the impending murder. He lay awake all night brooding about whether Ruttershields had a handwritten copy of his book, certain he would write it again, even if he hadn't.

Jane woke Dexter at 7.00 the following morning.

'I'll make coffee, Joss,' she said.

'Yes, go ahead and do that.'

Once Dexter had drunk three cups of coffee, his behaviour towards Jane became more amicable. She got back into bed.

'You did a wonderful job yesterday,' said Dexter.

Jane began to sulk.

'I know. What do I get in return?'

Dexter lit a cigarette.

'You'll get what your agency pays you. If you're a temporary secretary, the boss has to pay the agency for a full day, unless you fail to give satisfaction during the first three hours. That's not so in your case. The agency should pay you before Ruttershields finds out you've tampered with his work. That is what I mean by your reward.'

As he spoke, Dexter got out of bed and slowly put on his clothes.

Jane felt she had been taken for granted.

'Joss, I meant – what reward am I getting from you? I'm not talking about the agency. I risked my own personal safety. I could have been arrested.'

Dexter became irritable.

'What do you expect from me – a diamond tiara?'

'All I expect is a little appreciation,' said Jane quietly.

'Anyone would think we were man and wife!' snapped Dexter. 'Our relationship is not emotionally binding and never has been. It is purely sexual. I owe you nothing and unless you're prepared to accept my terms, you can get out now!'

Jane got up and dressed without speaking. She threw an ashtray at Dexter as she left.

'I don't ever want to see you again, Joss,' she said.

Dexter and Interkos met again the following evening in an obscure, Chinese restaurant at 6.00 p.m. They were the only customers. Dexter had brought the manuscript with him and handed it to Interkos who skimmed through it.

'This is bloody dynamite!' said Interkos.

'I know, but I've no evidence that Ruttershields doesn't have a handwritten copy of his manuscript locked away somewhere.'

Interkos struggled to use chopsticks. He asked for a knife and fork, irritated because they were not already on the table.

'You don't realise how lucky you are to have that girl,' said Interkos.

'We've split up. She expected too much of me. Our relationship wasn't serious from my point of view and she wasn't much of a lover either.'

Interkos gave an uncharacteristic, leering smile. He bent self-consciously over his rice.

'I bet she'd make a fabulous stiff,' he muttered conspiratorially.

'Good God, Douglas! I didn't know you were into "dead boring".'

'What FD isn't?' replied Interkos.

'FD? What's that?' asked Dexter.

'Funeral Director, of course. What do you think FD stands for?'

The following week, at 6.00 p.m., the two men met at another unoccupied restaurant.

'I've read the whole thing through,' said Interkos. 'We are left with no alternative but to kill Ruttershields. I'll go bust and so will you.'

Dexter thought for a while.

'What I do know for certain from my private dick is that he spends almost every night of the week in the Royal Society of Medicine, often with his punk lovers. As I've told you before, he has insomnia and has been seen walking about in the hall at any time between 4.00 and 6.00 a.m. That's the time and place to get him.'

Now that he realised the gravity of Dexter's mission, Interkos suddenly became nervous.

'Let's go over our roles. Who keeps him talking and who comes at him from behind?'

'As I told you, that's easily solved,' said Dexter. 'I'm a much more fluent speaker than you. I'll approach him as he walks about in the hall and I'll say I'm a journalist from the *British Medical Journal*. I'll show interest in his subject and ask a few journalistic questions.

'While I'm doing this, you will come up to him from behind with the mace and bash his brains in. We can't afford to be seen by bystanders in the street, even at that early hour. We will do what we have to do, take away the mace and go back to my room.'

'I don't understand why we should use such a crude and messy weapon as a mace,' said Interkos.

'That's a stupid remark. If we were to use something sophisticated, it would look as if an educated person had murdered him. If we use a mace, it's more likely to give the impression that one of Ruttershields's rough, punk lovers did it.'

'Yes, I see. In any event, I'm wearing gloves and I suggest you do, too.'

Dexter was getting bored with Interkos, his feminine, delicate sounding voice and his recurrent hypochondriasis.

'I'm not bothering with gloves,' he said irritably. 'I wear the bloody things all day.'

'All right,' said Interkos. 'Provided nothing untoward happens, the plan seems reasonable enough.'

Late on the evening of 2nd September, Dexter let Interkos into the Royal Society of Medicine with his key, carrying the mace in a bag in his left hand. The two men sat down on the street side of the receptionist's desk and waited. It was almost midnight when they sat down to wait for their quarry. It was going to be a long night so they both took the amphetamines which Dexter had provided.

They waited until 4.30 a.m. Ruttershields still had not come down to the hall.

Interkos began to lose faith.

'Is all this really worth it?' he asked in a whisper. 'What will we do if he isn't down by the time the building opens?'

Dexter got angry.

'I can't stand your perpetual pessimism. It's so typical of a suburban funeral director. If he comes down, he comes down. If he doesn't, we'll leave it till tomorrow.'

It wasn't until 6.45 a.m. that Ruttershields came out of the lift. He had obviously not expected to go back to sleep and was wearing his day clothes. By the time he walked to the receptionist's desk to leave the building, he was too bleary-eyed to notice Interkos springing behind him, clutching the mace in his gloved hand. Dexter rushed in front of him and addressed him with a charming smile.

'I'm sorry to trouble you, Professor Ruttershields. My name's James Rushton. I'm from the *British Medical Journal.* I've been reading about your plan to prolong youth and extend man's natural lifespan. I understand you're launching your book today. Do you mind if I ask you a few questions?'

Ruttershields was flattered and in his vanity failed to find it odd that a journalist should interview him so early in the morning.

'Why certainly, Mr Rushton.'

'Is it true, as a result of your research into ozone, that by the next century we will have discovered eternal life as well as eternal youth?'

'That would violate Newton's law of thermodynamics,' began Ruttershields.

Before he could finish, Interkos bounded forward from behind and swung the mace straight into his skull.

Ruttershields didn't die after one blow. It took Interkos at least four blows before his victim was lying dead, his brains spilling onto the marble floor.

Then the hearts of the two conspirators almost stopped dead. A sound was heard. They scrambled under the receptionist's desk and waited.

A woman holding a briefcase came out of the lift and into the hall. She stood still for a while as if she had forgotten something and went back to the lift. Dexter and Interkos had gone white.

'Come on, Joss, let's get out of here,' said Interkos.

'No, you brainless nincompoop – back to my room! We could be seen in the street. That woman will be back. Take the back stairs.'

In their hurry they left the mace behind.

The woman, a research assistant called Hilda Snelling, did not come back. She realised she had set her alarm two hours early and went back to sleep.

Once upstairs, Interkos went into Dexter's room and sat on his bed shaking. Dexter couldn't see any point in continuing his friendship with Interkos, who, although a reasonable golfing companion, was increasingly showing the tedious side of his personality with his whining voice and excessive preoccupation with his health.

Dexter eased himself under the bedclothes.

'Our mission is over. I don't think it wise for us to be seen in each other's company again.'

Interkos was humiliated.

'We are still friends, dammit. We can still play golf.'

Dexter kicked the bedclothes impatiently, jerking away Interkos's hand which was resting on them.

'No, we can't. As soon as this thing is over, I never want to see you or hear from you again. It would be dangerous. Besides, your company's not particularly scintillating.'

Interkos was so chafed by Dexter's words that he remained silent.

Eventually, he said, 'Nothing will stop me turning you in now. Just remember, I wore gloves. You did not. Your prints are on the handle of the mace, not mine and you were foolish enough to leave it by the body.'

Dexter, an inordinately unprofessional murderer, saw the logic of his co-conspirator and leapt out of bed in a violent rage. By now, they were standing on either side of the bed like the 'odd couple'. Dexter's words were no more than a whisper for fear of attracting attention.

'Ours was never a friendship. It just happened that we had a mutual need to protect our respective trades. Everything about you depresses me. It's mostly your trade, its trappings and the gloomy vulgarity of your offices. On top of that is your lack of conversational originality, your lukewarm sense of humour and your embarrassing behaviour in public. Not only that, you refer to funeral directors as FDs. No one else calls them that. Only you. I don't go round calling myself a PS, just because I'm a bloody plastic surgeon!'

'In what way has my behaviour in public been embarrassing?'

Dexter tried to light a cigarette. His lighter had run out of fuel. He swore under his breath and reached for a box of matches.

'I'm referring to that day when you walked round the golf course wearing a stethoscope.'

'I was worried. I had chest pains,' bleated Interkos.

'You're an exhibitionist. You're infantile. You're a bore! I'm sick of the sight of you, Douglas Intercourse!'

There was one thing and one thing only that hurt this proud, dignified, if eccentric Greek, and that was what he considered to be the prankish mis-pronunciation of his surname. He had endured it ever since his migration to England. He even had to tolerate it from some of his sniggering clients who sought comic relief in their time of bereavement.

He leant across the bed, staring lividly into Dexter's eyes and tore off the top sheet which he ripped in half in a homicidal rage.

'Don't you dare, ever again, address me as Douglas Intercourse when you know very well my name is Douglas Interkos!'

Dexter gripped him by the arm.

'Keep your foghorn down! We've just bumped someone off, or don't you remember?'

'We? We? Speak for yourself,' said Interkos, this time scarcely above a whisper. 'I wore gloves. You did not.'

'Shut up about your gloves. Just get as much distance between us as you can in the shortest amount of time.'

'All right. I won't waste my time seeing you again after the police arrive and check the building. However, I will say this: I've left no evidence on the murder weapon but you have, and because of your lack of loyalty towards me as a friend and because of your insults, including the intolerable mispronunciation of my surname, I can turn you in whenever feel like it.'

Interkos walked towards the door.

'So long Dexter, I'll make a public figure of you yet!'

He left to get what little sleep he could in the corridor.

Dexter gradually became aware of his predicament. He was terrified of going downstairs to retrieve the mace. He wished he hadn't been so destructive when complaining about Interkos's faults. It was true they should never meet again although he regretted his insults. He wondered whether Interkos would really turn him in and concluded, in the light of his remarks to him, that he probably would.

He got out a flask of whisky and took two swigs. Nothing could alter the fact that he had incompetently left his prints on the handle of the mace, which meant he would never get out of prison alive, whether Interkos turned him in or not.

'What can I do to see that Interkos doesn't turn me in?' Dexter said out loud.

He realised that his tension had caused him to go too far when speaking to Interkos. He wondered whether he should go and find him and withdraw his words. He smoked ten cigarettes before going out to look for him.

Dexter found Interkos asleep in the corridor.

'Hey, Doug.'

Interkos was jerked into consciousness from an exhausted sleep.

'What the hell do you want, Dexter?'

'Why are you lying in the corridor?'

'Because they wouldn't give me a room. What do you want?'

'Maybe I went over the top when I spoke to you before. I was under stress and I didn't mean a word I said,' said Dexter.

Interkos was still only half awake. Dexter was on

his knees by his supine body, making him look like a wounded soldier.

'I didn't mean to say any of those offensive things, Doug. I'll do anything I can to put things right between us.'

Interkos suddenly sat upright, banging his head against the wall. Dexter had a nervous giggling fit.

'For God's sake come back to my room. You can't afford to lie on the floor attracting attention to yourself.'

Once in his room, Dexter poured him a glass of whisky.

'OK, Doug, what do you want me to do? I'm not saying this just because I don't want you to turn me in. I know you've got too much decency to do that.'

Interkos stared distractedly into space, unable to think clearly due to lack of sleep.

'Just let me go to sleep, will you, Joss. I don't want to discuss anything now.'

Dexter had already taken the precaution of trying to salvage what he could of his inherited assets which were looked after by his father's trustees. He had also bought several boxes of black hair dye and an authentic-looking, false, black beard in case he suddenly had to leave the country. In addition, he had bribed an underworld acquaintance in South London to make up a false passport in the name of Jeremy Briggs.

Several weeks passed. Among the many others, Dexter and Interkos were called separately to the police station for questioning but neither was charged.

The conspirators kept out of each other's way and Interkos spent more time than before with his wife, Helena. As he watched her eating under the harsh, overhead light, it began to dawn on him how much her former beauty had deteriorated.

He remembered how stunning she had been in her youth with her red hair and flashing, black eyes. He recalled wistfully how drivers used to stop their cars to ogle her as she walked down the street.

Her cheekbones, once the most attractive feature of her face, were covered with brownish, sagging skin. Her smooth, taut complexion had been replaced by hollow jowls and she looked like a dismal, overweight troll. She knew what a spectacle she had become and never went out any more, even when Interkos wanted to take her out to dinner.

'Why don't you come out with me any more, Helena?'

'Take a look at me. I'd be ashamed to go out without a veil.'

Interkos brooded about her words and her opinion, which he shared. Because he no longer had Dexter to distract him, he allowed his initial thoughts to form themselves into a smouldering and agonising obsession.

He knew what he and his wife wanted. He summoned the courage to ring Dexter.

'Joss? Are you free to speak?'

'Yes. Hullo, Douglas. What can I do for you?'

Interkos lit a cigarette.

'You know you said that if there was anything I wanted you to do, you would do it?'

'Well, within reason. What *do* you want?'

'Have you ever seen my wife?' asked Interkos nervously.

'Yes, briefly. She's got red hair, hasn't she?'

'Yes, she was beautiful in her youth, but because she has become so hideous with age, she won't go out and hides herself from visitors.'

'Get to the point, Douglas. What you're trying to say is that you want me to lift her face.'

Interkos deeply inhaled smoke into his lungs.

'That's about right. She and I have discussed the possibility of a facelift and she wants to have it done as much as I do.'

Dexter paused for a while.

'I'll do that for you, old boy.'

'How much will it cost?'

'If you're a good boy, I'll do it free of charge.'

Dexter got blind drunk the night before doing Mrs Interkos's facelift. He didn't really want to do it but did so out of fear that Interkos would turn him in.

As Mrs Interkos's sedated mass of quivering blubber was wheeled into the operating theatre, Dexter's hangover was so bad that he had to suppress the urge to retch. He turned to the nurse.

'Scalpel, sweetie.'

His shaking, rubber-gloved hand cut an incision just above Mrs Interkos's hairline. She had so much fat on the top few layers of her facial skin that

Dexter found it difficult to distinguish between fat and nerves.

He stretched the skin until it was taut, but in scraping the fat off the skin, he inadvertently severed a vital nerve. Realising his mistake, Dexter decided that his only hope would be to leave the country as soon as possible.

As he struggled to keep the bile from his mouth, he stitched the taut skin back under the hairline and bandaged the woman's head.

By the time the bandages were removed, Dexter had only just managed to salvage some of his unearned assets which were enough for him to live on, if not indefinitely.

The clinic rang Interkos to tell him that the bandages would be removed from his wife's face that day. In his obsessive state, Interkos left a funeral prematurely and drove the hearse to the clinic like a maniac, still wearing his funeral clothes. He rammed the hearse onto a pavement in Harley Street, and screeched it to a halt, leaving it unlocked with the key in the ignition.

His wife's bandages had already been removed. One side of her face sagged even more than it had before. The other side made her look like an eighteen-year-old girl. Her eye on the damaged part of her face looked like a dead fish on a slab. The other eye was sparkling and full of girlish allure. She looked as if she had suffered a massive stroke.

Interkos fainted.

* * *

It took Interkos 15 minutes to become orientated. When he did, he found his way to Dexter's office.

Dexter had the foresight to block the door, the lock of which was broken, and clutched a golf club in his hand in case Interkos broke the door down. In the meantime, a clanging stretcher was being wheeled past Dexter's office. Interkos ignored it. For the first time in his life, he raised his gentle voice to a menacing roar.

'I know you're in there, Joss Dexter!'

One of the porters wheeling the trolley thought he was hallucinating on seeing this furious man in funereal attire banging on Dexter's door in a rage.

'Come out and face me, Joss Dexter, you sick bastard!'

Dexter was silent.

'If you don't answer, I'm breaking this door down.'

Both the porters were too stunned and in too much of a hurry to tell him to be quiet and leave.

Interkos heaved his weight against the door until it gave way. Dexter knocked off his top hat and hit him repeatedly over the head with the golf club, killing him outright.

It took Dexter at least three minutes to realise that he had committed another murder. He was so stunned that he took several swigs from the whisky flask he carried in his pocket.

The door had been broken down and he couldn't lock it from the inside, so he pushed over the heavy, oak writing desk to prevent anyone coming in. Then he dragged Interkos's body beneath his consulting couch and wiped away as much of the blood as he could with paper and water from the sink.

He pulled out a box of black hair dye which he carried in one of his briefcases. He removed his surgeon's overalls, went to the sink and pushed his head under the tap. Then he smothered the dye over his hair and waited for 20 minutes for the new colour to take hold before putting the empty box into his briefcase.

He bundled his overalls into a ball and left them by Interkos's body under the couch. He put on his dark, pinstriped suit. He dried his hair carefully, glued on the false, black beard and was impressed by its authenticity. He picked up his two briefcases, one containing the spare boxes of hair dye and the false passport, and the other containing £20,000 in bank notes taken from his family trust.

He estimated that it would take a little while for Interkos's body to be discovered. He cleaned the room up, moved the oak desk blocking the door and turned off the anglepoise lamp. Finally, in order to confuse his pursuers, he left a scrawled note on the desk saying, 'Have gone away to end it all.'

Then he opened the door to make sure no one was outside, left the room, his appearance now completely unrecognisable, and walked out of the building whistling.

Within half an hour, he had boarded a train for the coast.

* * *

91

It was not until the following morning that Interkos's body was found, followed by a nationwide alert and the publication of a photograph of Dexter's cherubic face on the front page of every national newspaper. By this time, he had already left the country.

The task of Detective Inspector Massey and Detective Constable Bush was not made easy by the fact that only two witnesses saw Interkos breaking into Dexter's office. Neither of them saw Dexter himself. The two stretcher-bearers were David Atkins, who actually saw Interkos more closely because he was facing him, and Cyril Anderson who only caught a fleeting glimpse of him as he was going through the door.

Massey questioned Atkins.

'Would you mind telling us exactly what you saw?'

'I thought I saw this bloke dressed up as an undertaker, screaming and shouting, trying to break down a door.'

'I'm not interested in what you thought you saw. I want to know what you did see,' said Massey with the marked lack of manners characteristic of him.

'Well, I'm sure that's what I saw but it could have been a hallucination. I'd had a beer or two. It was my birthday.'

'Do you normally drink before you go on duty?'

'No. It was only on that occasion.'

'Did it not occur to you to approach this man breaking into someone's office and say, "Can I help you"?'

'No, of course it didn't,' said Atkins. 'The patient on the stretcher had had a heart attack. It was a bleeding emergency.'

'Couldn't you have spoken to him while you

continued to wheel the patient down the corridor?'

'Are you suggesting I could have delayed things by asking an undertaker if I could help him? He would probably have said, "You bet you can, Guv. Hand that over. It looks like a croaker"!'

Massey went purple with rage and banged his fist down on his knee.

'Don't mess about with me, wasting my time making silly jokes! Did you see anyone behind the door once the man had broken in?'

'No one at all.'

'You said the man was screaming and shouting. What did he say?'

'He said, "I know you're in there, Joss Dexter. Come out and face me, you sick bastard!"'

'Did Dexter answer?'

'If he did, I didn't hear anything.'

'Do you know Dexter?'

'No. I've never met him in my life. Just because I was rushing past his office, it doesn't mean to say I knew him. I didn't even know who he was until all this blew up.'

Dexter's office was checked for fingerprints. Those of Dexter, which covered a large part of the oak desk and other objects in the office, were found to match the prints on the handle of the mace which had killed Ruttershields.

It was Massey who broke the news of Interkos's death to Helena Interkos as she lay recuperating just after her bandages had been removed. It was a fortunate coincidence that Massey had broken the news before she had access to a mirror.

*   *   *

Massey and Bush were discussing their latest findings at the police station.

'I've got a pretty good idea what happened,' said Massey. 'Interkos and Dexter must have been in this together. Ruttershields's handwritten notes referred to this so-called, ozone formula which could prolong youth and postpone decay. Hence, he was a hindrance to both their livelihoods. The fact that Dexter was involved is substantiated by the matching prints. I'm surprised he was so amateurish and didn't wear gloves.

'Presumably, they quarrelled after the murder. Interkos may have threatened to turn him in, and Dexter, in a desperate effort to avoid this, must have offered to give Interkos's wife a facelift.

'Dexter was obviously under a lot of stress which made him unduly careless on the job. He destroyed that woman's face beyond chances of even elementary repair. Once Interkos saw what Dexter had done, he stormed into his office, presumably intending to kill him, but Dexter battered him to death before he had a chance.

'No one saw him leave. I can't be sure the suicide note he left was genuine. He may have been trying to put us all off his trail.'

Bush was confused by Massey's complicated version of events. He felt self-conscious about his inferior intellect and slower brain than that of his superior colleague, as well as feeling intensely intimidated.

'Sounds a most interesting and substantial theory, sir,' he muttered.

94

'It's more than that, Bush,' said Massey irritably. 'Here's this degenerate genius who could prolong youth and postpone death. Wouldn't you feel you had to do something about it if you were either a plastic surgeon or a funeral director?'

Bush ran his hand through his hair and cleared his throat.

'If it were me, I'd abandon my trade and retrain for another profession,' he replied, spontaneously showing an ingrained instinct for honesty.

'Don't be so daft, Bush!' snarled Massey.

It took the police three days to find Dexter's father, Jeff, and his brother, Joe. Joe had accompanied his father who had been conducting an orchestra at the Edinburgh Festival Hall. The father and son had returned to their London house where Joe, a lecturer, occupied a basement flat and joined his father for dinner most evenings.

It was 11.00 p.m. They were about to go to bed when the doorbell rang. Jeff opened the door and found Massey and Bush who introduced themselves.

'Are you Mr Jeffrey Dexter, the father of Joshua Dexter, the surgeon?' asked Massey.

Jeff whitened and felt as if he were about to faint, fearing his son was dead.

'Yes.'

'I'm afraid we have some very startling news. May we come in?'

Jeff walked backwards into the hall and gripped the bannister for support. He ushered Massey and

Bush into the living room where Joe was drinking whisky. Jeff stretched out his hand in a subservient gesture, unable to speak. He staggered to an armchair and sat down, leaning forwards with his hands, palms downwards, on his knees.

'What's happened to Joss?' he asked hoarsely.

Massey decided to be as succinct as it was possible to be when telling such a complex and bizarre story.

'Mr Dexter has disappeared from the hospital where he works. He left a note on his desk, which read, "Have gone away to end it all." A dead body was found concealed in his office and it has been identified as that of a funeral director called Douglas Interkos. We believe he got into a fight with your son and was killed. Your son had just operated on his wife's face. He had an accident and disfigured her for life, which is probably why the fight took place.'

Jeff leant back in his chair, his head tilted backwards and his mouth gaping open like a cadaver's. Joe rushed to his side with half a glass of neat whisky which he poured into his father's mouth.

Eventually, Jeff was able to speak.

'Is my son still alive? That's all I want to know! Is he still alive?'

'I'm afraid I don't know, sir,' said Massey with uncharacteristic gentleness. 'The suicide note may not have been genuine. Mr Dexter may not have been intending to take his life at all. It could be that he left the note to fool us. Do you know him to be a suicidal type of person?'

Jeff took another swig of whisky.

'I wouldn't for one moment say my son has suicidal tendencies. There's no chance he could have taken his life, whatever mess he had got himself into. He's never had melancholic tendencies. He's far too frivolous and pleasure-loving to be the brooding type. My Joss loves life. He always has.'

He was about to say something else but tailed off. He burst into tears. Joe put his arm round him.

'Mr Dexter, I know how deeply distressing this is for you, but I do have to ask you a few questions. When did you last see your son?' asked Massey.

'Quite some time ago. We had lunch together on 2nd September. I remember the date because it was the day before there was all that publicity about the man who was murdered in the Royal Society of Medicine.'

'When you had lunch, how did your son seem to you? Can you remember what sort of a mood he was in?'

Jeff thought for a while. His speech was becoming slurred.

'Oddly enough, he didn't seem in a particularly good mood. He wasn't as relaxed as he normally is. He was very affectionate as always, but he wasn't his cocky, ebullient self. He was drinking quite a lot. He was very fidgety and was off his food. He was like a boy about to take an examination.'

'Did you ask him if there was anything wrong?'

'No. I didn't want to because it was clear he was trying to hide his anxiety from me.'

'Does he usually come to you with his problems?'

'Never, not Joss. He's always very kind to me but

he tells me nothing, not even about his work. I know he's always chasing women but he's never introduced any of his girlfriends to his family. His right hand doesn't know what his left hand is doing. Oh, God, I hope he's all right!'

Another fit of sobbing, exacerbated by the whisky, seized Jeff. Joe embraced him, allowing his father's head to rest on his shoulder.

'Of course Joss is all right,' he said. 'He's a survivor. He's hiding somewhere. Besides, even if the man he fought with did accidentally get killed, the worst that could happen would be a manslaughter charge.'

Massey interrupted.

'Mr Dexter, do you happen to know whether your son knew Professor Ruttershields, who was murdered at the Royal Society of Medicine?'

'I doubt it.'

'Why?'

'Because, although Joss seldom talks about his work, the people he would be most likely to associate with would be other surgeons, not fringe quacks like Ruttershields.'

Suddenly, Jeff rolled off the armchair onto the floor in a faint and was unconscious for about a minute. Massey and Bush got up to leave and said they would have to return another time.

'You take it easy with him next time,' said Joe, his voice raised in anger. 'My father's not that young and I won't tolerate his being made ill again.'

'I'm sorry, sir,' said Bush, who spoke for the first time during the interview. 'We are only doing our duty.'

'Well go and do your duty somewhere else and don't come here making my father ill!' shouted Joe.

The police called the following evening at 6.00 p.m. Joe was in but Jeff had gone out for a walk. Massey was relieved that he did not have to break the unpleasant news to the older man personally. He was exhausted and unwilling to take responsibility for causing Jeff to faint a second time.

Jeff returned to the house at 7.30 p.m. and was greeted in the hall by Joe who guided him to his armchair in the living room.

'The police came back when you were out.'

'What did they say?'

'They didn't say Joss had come to harm.'

Jeff immediately relaxed, believing no further information could possibly jolt him. He leant back in his chair.

'I'm afraid you must prepare yourself for a shock,' said Joe.

'All right, get on with it.'

'The police said the fingerprints on the handle of the mace which killed Ruttershields were the same as the prints in Joss's office, as well as on his personal possessions.'

Jeff let out a strange, unearthly, croaking groan. It was a heart attack. He died instantly.

Joe was shattered, both by his father's sudden death and by the disappearance of his brother, to whom he had always been close and who was suspected of committing two murders. He threw himself into his work and waited for news of his brother.

Some months passed. He had received two calls from the police about Joss's whereabouts, both of which turned out to be bogus. One police caller stated that a blond-haired man bearing an identical resemblance to Joss had been found and arrested in a Johannesburg nightclub, only to be released after four hours. Joe was later informed that Joss had been found in Australia, where a man had been remanded until his true identity was discovered.

One sultry August evening in Marseilles, a drunk strode arrogantly into a bar overlooking the harbour. The man was unkempt with inky, black hair and a thick, inky, black beard which covered most of his face. The only endearing feature of his face was a pair of large, liquid-grey eyes which were permanently feasted on women.

He wore black shoes, tight-fitting jeans and a white, open-necked shirt.

The bar was called La Tosca. It was crowded with tough-looking, off-duty legionnaires, some of whom had brought loose women along with them.

As he entered the bar, the man looked briefly from woman to woman, stumbled over a chair and approached the counter.

The legionnaires did not like the look of this man because of the lecherous manner in which he ogled their latest conquests.

The man had to wait for a while for someone to serve him. His drunken state was making him aggressive. He banged his fist on the counter.

'*Je cherche une femme!*' he bellowed.

The bartender, a well-built man wearing a white blazer and a bow tie, vaulted over the counter, punched the newcomer in the jaw and bundled him into the street. After a few minutes, the man, still in an advanced state of drunkenness, staggered back to his hotel.

The Hôtel Méditeranné, where he had been living for several months, was a charming, old hotel overlooking the harbour. It was owned by two elderly brothers who took it in turns to man the small reception area. Their names were Marcel and Alphonse and they had both taken a liking to their long-term customer, whom they knew as Jeremy Briggs, the name used by Joss Dexter.

That night, Alphonse was on duty.

'What happened, Monsieur Briggs? Are you all right?'

'Yes, I'm fine. A man attacked me in the street, that's all.'

Alphonse had been charmed by Dexter, who paid his bills regularly and spoke French perfectly, as well as being courteous, genial and friendly. Neither brother minded when sex-obsessed Dexter took women to his room. Indeed, they admired his energy which reminded them of their youth.

'Are you sure you're all right? How about some coffee?'

'No, thank you. I'm fine. I've had a bit too much to drink. I'll go up and sleep it off.'

Dexter had always been enchanted by Marseilles, ever since he visited the city as a child, accompanied by Joe, Jeff and his mother, Sylvia, shortly before she died. He had been there on several occasions in adulthood and had taken his girlfriends with him when he stayed at a five-star hotel by the harbour.

The city held a fascinating and passionate attraction for him. He loved its seediness, its bouillabaisse restaurants surrounding the harbour, its back streets cluttered with old syringes, its wafts of garlic, the permanent sound of an accordion and the colourful street fights occurring near the harbour and in the alleys. Most of all, he loved to swim round the harbour and watch the sunset, followed by the reflection of the city's lights on the water.

Dexter couldn't sleep the night he was thrown out of the bar. He got up and sat in a café, drinking hot chocolate and cognac. As he went back to the hotel, Alphonse noticed he had an out-of-date English newspaper under his arm and that he had been crying.

'Monsieur Briggs, is there anything I can do to help?'

Alphonse's kind words caused him to start crying again. The older man came out into the reception area and put his hand on Dexter's shoulder.

'What is it, monsieur?'

Dexter threw his arms round Alphonse and sobbed like a child.

'I heard only this afternoon that my father died some months ago!'

'Your father? I'm so sorry. Did he die in England?'

'Yes.'

'Then you will want to go home and be with your family?'

'I'm never going home, Alphonse! I'm never going home!'

Once in his room, Dexter read about his father's death. The article, accompanied by a flattering photograph of Dexter, was splashed over the front page of the *Daily Mail*. It described in detail how Jeff had had a sudden heart attack on hearing that his son was a prime murder suspect. The main theme of the article was the exasperation of the police through failing to find Dexter after such a long passage of time.

For the next week, Dexter drank alone in his room and had his meals brought to him by Alphonse who was becoming a surrogate father.

'Go on, Monsieur Briggs, go out and find a woman. It will do you good,' said Alphonse when bringing him his dinner one evening.

Dexter was at an advantage in that there was a fine network of disorderly houses outside the hotel.

He took Alphonse's advice. As he increased his pleasures, so he decreased his grief and guilt. Each morning, he had coffee and hot croissants which he ate at a table by the window, taking in the magnificent view of the harbour. At midday, he forced himself to buy the English newspapers which he read in a café, taking the edge off their harrowing contents with a bottle of whisky. Once his guilt was anaesthetised, he removed his clothes and plunged into the harbour and swam round it with an energetic crawl.

Each day, he had a gourmet lunch after his swim, picked up a prostitute and either went to her room or brought her back to the hotel. Then he slept for two hours before going on his evening swim round the harbour, followed by dinner.

He was able to swim until October. In the winter months, he took less exercise, more women and more sleep. He realised that his money would not last indefinitely, having taken his decadent lifestyle for granted. He knew he would have to move out of the hotel and into a boarding house away from the harbour if he still intended to buy sex, which he couldn't do without.

His predicament did not seem particularly daunting at the time, but once he left Alphonse to move into a small, single room, containing a cooker, a bidet and a sink, he became aware of how acutely lonely and miserable he was.

His room was on the ground floor of a run-down, three-storey house in an Algerian ghetto. It looked onto a gloomy courtyard with clothes lines across it. The foul-smelling, seldom collected litter in the small hall outside his room diminished his macabre fascination for the seamy side of life in Marseilles. The walls of the hall were covered with ancient, peeling posters saying *Algérie Française*. In a corner was a lavatory of indescribable filthiness used by all the occupants of the building.

For a reason he couldn't understand, Dexter began to feel exhausted and became much thinner. He slept until midday, summoned the energy to get something to eat in a café and went back to bed.

As the months passed, his fatigue increased. He no longer even had the energy to chase women.

One bleak, wintry morning, he was woken by a knock on the door. Instinctively, he feared it was the police. He put on a woman's voice.

'Who is it?'

He was surprised when the voice answered in English.

'May I come in?'

'Who are you? What do you want?'

'There's no need to be aggressive. I'm your neighbour. I live on the first floor. I heard you're the only other Englishman in the building.'

Dexter eased himself out of bed, alarmed by his increased weakness. He staggered to the door and opened it.

'Come in,' he muttered.

The man who stood before him was six foot tall, bald and wearing a blue boiler suit. He stretched out his hand.

'My name's Martin Wesley. It's nice to meet a fellow countryman abroad. I'm an engineer.'

'My name's Jeremy Briggs. I'm afraid I'm not very well so I'm going to lie down.'

Wesley looked round Dexter's filthy room. There was a pile of unwashed plates in the sink, unlaundered clothes on the floor and an unemptied bucket encircled by flies used as a lavatory.

'May I sit on your bed?'

'Yes, all right, but I can't let you stay for long because I'm going back to sleep. Why are you in Marseilles?'

Wesley sat down gently, aware of Dexter's frailty.

'I've lived here all my life. My mother was French. I can't imagine living anywhere else. And you?'

'I've settled down here because I can't afford to pay alimony to my wife and daughter. I have a particular love for this city but I never thought I'd end up in a place like this. Are you married?'

'No. I'm divorced. My wife's dead now. Road accident. No children.'

'Would you think it very rude if I went back to sleep? Perhaps we can talk later.'

'I'd like that,' said Wesley. 'What's wrong with you, if I might ask?'

'I've no idea and I don't want to find out. I'm afraid you must go now. I don't mean to be abrupt but I really do feel dreadful.'

'Do you want a doctor?'

Dexter was beginning to feel irritated. He saw Wesley as being a kind person and struggled to keep his temper.

'No. Maybe if I get worse, I'll ask you to get one. Thanks anyway.'

Wesley called in to see Dexter every morning before he went out. Dexter was torn between irritation at having another man's company imposed on him, and comfort through the knowledge that he could be helped and consoled if he became iller.

One morning, Wesley found that Dexter had deteriorated dramatically. His weight had plummeted to seven stone and he had diarrhoea and pneumonia.

Wesley went through the disagreeable procedure of emptying Dexter's overflowing bucket and returned to the filthy, fly-infested room.

'I'm going to have to get a doctor, Jeremy. I can't take responsibility for leaving you in this state.'

'All right,' muttered Dexter, his voice scarcely above a whisper, 'but make sure it's a French doctor.'

Wesley looked baffled.

'I've got a very good English doctor called Dr Duggan. He used to look after my parents.'

Dexter struggled to sit up in bed but failed. He noticed for the first time that his emaciated arms were covered with suppurating lesions.

'I'm not seeing a bloody English doctor, do you hear?'

'Why on earth not?'

'Because English doctors are no good. I've seen enough of them in the past.'

'It's Dr Duggan or nothing,' said Wesley firmly.

A wave of fear surged through Dexter. The idea of being recognised by a reader of English newspapers and being deported when he was so ill, was unbearable to him.

'All right. I'll agree to it but before you get this man out, will you do one thing for me?'

'Of course. What?'

Dexter laboriously turned on his side to avoid having to look at Wesley.

'This may seem odd but I'm terribly self-conscious about my white hair growing out at the roots. I don't want anyone to see it as it's something I really care about. Will you go to a chemist and buy me some black dye?'

Wesley was astounded.

'Well, I will if you insist, but it's hardly a priority.'

'It is to me, Martin.'

Wesley failed to understand why a man so ill and living in such squalor would be vain enough to wish to dye his hair just because he was going to see a doctor, but he recognised that Dexter was a stubborn, private, intensely peculiar person who was not to be contradicted.

'All right. I'll be back in half an hour with the dye. Then I'll get Duggan out.'

'Thanks, Martin. Don't think I don't appreciate your kindness.'

Wesley returned with three boxes of black dye, assuming the procedure would have to be repeated. He pulled back the bedclothes, lifted Dexter and turned him round so that his head tilted backwards over the front of the bed.

He got a basin from his room, returned to Dexter and filled the basin with hot water which he bathed over Dexter's hair. Then he squeezed the dye from the tube and smothered it over his head, leaving it on for 20 minutes. He washed it off after filling the basin three times. He then wrapped Dexter's head in a towel and picked him up and laid him in his original position.

'I'm going to call Duggan out now.'

The phone at Duggan's practice took some time to answer. Wesley stressed the urgency of the case and was told that Duggan's partner, Dr Ross, would come to see Dexter as Duggan was out making calls.

Dr Ross was a short, stockily-built, sharp-featured

man with a crewcut. Wesley let him in to Dexter's room. Dexter was lying, half out of bed, making an effort to suck air into his lungs, clasping his chest with his lesion-infested arms. Dr Ross gaped at him in alarm and turned to Wesley.

'May I have a word with you in the hall?'

'Yes. Why?'

'Forgive me for asking but have you been having any sexual relations with your friend?'

'No. Certainly not. I don't understand.'

'Good. Will you wait here while I take a look at him.'

Ross put on a pair of rubber gloves and examined Dexter.

'How long have you been ill, sir?'

'I started feeling ill months and months ago but I got worse two days ago.'

'Can you tell me when you last had sexual relations?'

'Not since I started feeling ill.'

'May I ask if you had a lot of different partners?'

'Yes. I was having up to three prostitutes a day. My sex drive was so overpowering I couldn't do without.'

'Have you had relations with any men?'

'Good God no! I'm a tits and pussy man, myself.'

Ross cleared his throat. He stroked the side of his face as he searched for words, appalled by the disgusting state of the room and fearing instinctively for his own health.

'It's AIDS, isn't it, Doc?' said Dexter.

'Yes, sir, it looks as if it is,' replied Ross hoarsely.

'How long do you think I've got?'

'The illness is in a very advanced state. I'd say

you only have a few months. Is your friend able to look after you?'

'Yes. I'd rather die here than go near a hospital.'

'Technically, you should be in hospital but I can't force you. I'm going to give you some antibiotics for your pneumonia and something else for your diarrhoea. You should improve and will probably feel well enough to get up and go out within a few weeks. However, this will not last. You will become ill again because of the very nature of the disease.'

Ross put his examining instruments back into his bag and went out into the hall to meet Wesley.

'What's the matter with him, Dr Ross?'

'Your friend is very seriously ill. He's dying.'

'Dying? Of what?'

'He has all the symptoms of full-blown AIDS. I give him a few months.'

Wesley was too startled to speak straight away.

'Of course, he'd be much better off in hospital but he refuses to be admitted. I've prescribed him some antibiotics for his pneumonia. Are you able to look after him?'

'Of course I am. I'll stay with him till the end. You can be sure of that.'

'I understand my partner, Dr Duggan, looked after your parents.'

'Yes, that's right.'

'It's so nice to come across English people once in a while, isn't it?' I used to buy all the English newspapers but I've stopped now. I'm so sick and tired of that story about the surgeon who killed the funeral director.'

'What surgeon?' asked Wesley.

'Don't you know? His name's Joss Dexter. The papers have bored me stiff writing about him. The police are still looking for him. Anyway, I'll call in again tomorrow.'

When Wesley went back into Dexter's room, he was alarmed by the terrified expression on his face.

'Don't look so worried. I'm going to look after you.'

'I couldn't help hearing the conversation between you and the doctor in the hall.'

'There's nothing he hasn't told you personally.' Dexter tried to sound casual.

'I happened to overhear him mention Joss Dexter who's on the run. Did I hear him say the police were still after him?'

'Yes, that's right. Why are you so interested?'

'Because it's an absolutely fascinating story. It's my guess Dexter's committed suicide. Otherwise, they'd have found him, wouldn't they? What do you think?'

'I don't know and I don't care,' said Wesley.

During the course of the next two months, Dexter's pneumonia gradually improved. Wesley cleaned his room, tidied away his clothes, washed his plates with hot water and disinfectant and emptied his bucket, the latter procedure being necessary twice a day. He cooked him a bowl of porridge and treacle for breakfast and came home from work to give him soup and bread for lunch and the same for dinner, which Dexter forced himself to eat so as not to hurt Wesley's feelings.

'I must say you're looking better today,' said Wesley one morning, as he brought Dexter his porridge.

'I feel a bit better.'

It was an exceptionally warm spring day. The midday sun was as hot as that of an English summer.

'Do you know what I'd like to do?'

'What?' asked Wesley.

'I'd like it if you could take me out in the wheelchair, drive me to the streets leading to the harbour and let me look at the women.'

'I don't see why not, but we shouldn't be out for more than an hour or two.'

Wesley wrapped Dexter up in rugs and carried him to his scruffy but tough-looking Citreon 2CV, into which he placed him gently in the passenger seat, before folding up the wheelchair and putting it in the boot. They drove along the harbour, past the Hôtel Méditeranné and parked in a back street. Wesley lifted Dexter out of the car, lowered him into the wheelchair and pushed him along the rue St Farréol which was lined with prostitutes. Dexter's voice was scarcely above a whisper.

'I could drink this in as if it were wine.'

'Perhaps it is.'

As he saw a peroxide blonde woman in a tight-fitting, leopard-skin dress and white, high-heeled boots, his lips parted in a smile. He was unaware of the fact that his swollen, bleeding gums had covered his teeth, making him look like a freak.

'Oh, Martin, I want them so badly. To see them gives me so much joy and yet so much pain.'

The leopard-skin clad prostitute gripped her friend standing beside her by the wrist.

'Keep away from him! He's got AIDS.'

Wesley could bear it no longer and was seized by a sudden surge of anger.

'Yes, he has and it's one of you bitches who gave it to him!'

Dexter was struck by the coarseness of Martin's Marseilles accent in comparison with his refined, English vowels.

'Don't get angry, Martin. They're all so beautiful. Do you realise that really elegant women copy prostitutes when they dress?'

Wesley noticed that Dexter was crying, like a child that yearned for something it couldn't have.

'Come on, you're getting tired. I'll take you home.'

'Do you know something? If Joss Dexter happened to be in Marseilles, I'm sure this is the first place he'd go to.'

'Do stop going on about bloody Joss Dexter! We're going home.'

As spring progressed to summer, Wesley took Dexter out almost every day. He was continuously losing weight and deteriorating and although he knew he was dying, he felt an extraordinary sense of euphoria because he had managed to live another day.

When he was wheeled past the prostitutes for two hours every afternoon, he felt like a prisoner being let out of his cell, if only to see the light of day. Once he was taken home, he would lie awake counting the hours until he would next be taken out.

Wesley was carrying him to the car.

'Why do you always have to be so nice to me, Martin?'

'Because, until I met you I was lonely. I wasn't seeing anyone from one day to the next. I was sorry for you and I wanted to look after you.'

'But I'm an invalid. Soon I'll be dead. What companionship can I possibly offer you to alleviate your loneliness?'

'You've got yourself to offer. Whether or not you're ill is neither here nor there.'

'How will you manage when I'm dead?'

Wesley lifted Dexter into the car.

'Don't worry about me. I'm sure I'll find another invalid to look after.'

These words, delivered as a joke, tormented Dexter who momentarily thought Wesley was mocking his former indiscretions.

The visit to the prostitutes was less happy that afternoon than on previous occasions. The two men had been moving along the same streets with almost clockwork regularity and had become well known to the women. They closed in on Wesley and Dexter chanting. '*Pédés d'année! Pédés d'année!*'*

'I'm getting you away from here,' said Wesley.

'It doesn't matter. Do let's stay. They'll get bored with us after a time and they'll ignore us.'

---

* 'Queers of the year!'

114

They stayed on the pavement of the rue St Farréol. Gradually, the women left and returned to their rooms. Dexter felt like a child robbed of its toys and wept.

'I'll get a loaf of bread to feed the gulls and we can go for a walk near the harbour before we go home,' said Wesley.

They went as far as the harbour entrance, Dexter's favourite part of the harbour because of its superb view. Children climbed onto the sharp, white stones leading to the water. Dexter feebly threw bread to the gulls as he watched the children swimming round the moored boats.

'Come on, Jeremy, you've had enough for one day,' said Wesley.

Within the next few days, Dexter's health deteriorated further. His weight had plummeted to five stone and his bones protruded like a famine victim's. Wesley slept on a mattress on the floor of his room, certain he was going to die during the night.

He lasted for another day. He was too weak to raise his hand to attract Wesley's attention and spoke in a hoarse whisper.

'Martin, I can see the sun setting on the walls through the window. Something tells me this is the last sunset I'll ever see. Will you take me to the harbour entrance?'

Wesley did as he was asked. The setting sun shone on the buildings surrounding the harbour, giving them a gentle, mellow, pinkish hue.

'Will you lie me on my stomach with my head facing the harbour.'

Wesley lifted Dexter and laid him down. He weighed no more than a tiny, little doll.

'I've just noticed something extraordinary about your hair,' said Wesley. 'It isn't white growing out at the roots. It's blond. It's a lovely colour. Why on earth do you insist on having it dyed black?'

Dexter raised his head with a superhuman effort. He allowed his eyes to scan the pink buildings surrounding the harbour as he spoke, knowing this was the last time he would see them.

'Because I am Joss Dexter, the surgeon,' he said.

Dexter lowered his head and let his face rest on the flagstone and drifted into eternal sleep.

Wesley broke up the loaf of bread he had brought with him and threw the pieces to the gulls.